STAR TREK

THE
KLINGON EMPIRE

STAR TREK™

THE
KLINGON EMPIRE

DAYTON WARD

ILLUSTRATIONS BY
LIVIO RAMONDELLI AND PETER MARKOWSKI

INSIGHT ◉ EDITIONS

San Rafael, California

CONTENTS

INTRODUCTION

tlhIngan maH!*

You have chosen to embark on a quest of discovery, perhaps while seeking to test your own mettle and determine your worthiness to visit one of the Galaxy's most formidable and perhaps misunderstood civilizations.

At one time, offworlders venturing into our Empire—let alone setting foot on our home world—would have been met with the full force of our armies. The very idea that Klingons might do anything but subjugate or simply annihilate such interlopers would be absurd. However, my prolonged exposure to the humans of Earth and others who wrap themselves in the banner of the Federation has served to modify many views I once held as absolute.

Though we are a race of warriors, driven to conquest and victory in battle, we understand and appreciate the value of trusted allies. This includes welcoming them to the Homeworld. It fascinates me that those we once called enemies are so eager to journey here in order to experience firsthand our people and our culture. For centuries, we expended great effort to protect our world from the scrutiny of outsiders, even as we pushed ever outward in our quest to expand our borders and accumulate resources. Only in recent decades have we allowed that veil of isolation to be lifted.

Qo'noS is the beating heart of the Empire, and our world possesses a long and tumultuous history. From violent, even chaotic, beginnings grew a civilization that has become both respected and feared throughout the stars. As a visitor among us, you are invited to explore and discover what it means to be Klingon. Contrary to popular belief, we are not simply a race of warriors. While it is true that military strength has always been a primary focus for our people, no civilization can exist without scientists, doctors, engineers, and even artists. Just as we can forge weapons of war, so too can we shape the minds of our youth through science and technology, as well as literature and philosophy.

You will learn in short order that we Klingons are a proud, boisterous people. In the past, we have been reticent about interacting with other species unless we were fighting or conquering them. That attitude has shifted in recent generations—albeit in very measured degrees—and I have no doubt that our prolonged relationship with the Federation has helped modify this outlook. But make no mistake: Klingons are Klingons. We cherish our heritage and will vigorously defend it against those who would bring it dishonor; however, we also are increasingly willing to share our culture with those eager to understand our ways.

I urge you to seize every opportunity to experience our way of life. You'll discover that we abide by numerous traditions, many of them handed down through the centuries so that we never forget our history or our destiny. Enjoy your stay with us, traveler, and learn from it. The Klingon Empire awaits you.

*Qapla'!***
Martok, Chancellor of the Klingon High Council
August 2387 (Federation standard calendar)

* We are Klingons!
** Success!

WELCOME TO QO'NOS

"Hem tlhIngan Segh 'ej maHemtaH 'e' wlHech."
("Klingons are a proud race, and we intend to go on being proud.")
—Azetbur, Chancellor to the Klingon High Council, 2293

GETTING HERE

Qo'noS is located in the Klinzhai Star System and is the center of the Klingon Empire. The planet features a single landmass, which boasts a variety of rugged terrain that might be considered uninviting to all but the hardiest of offworlders. Though Qo'noS accepts visitors throughout most of its calendar year, travelers are advised to be aware of various celebrations and cultural observances, including several that are off-limits to non-Klingons. For more details, consult your travel guide or one of the many visitor assistance centers located around the planet.

When planning your trip, don't forget that Qo'noS is but one planet within the Empire. We understand it's likely to be the focal point of any vacation in Klingon territory, but be sure to take advantage of the various side trip opportunities. Imperial rule extends to more than thirty worlds, spread over a dozen star systems. A few of these planets were initially uninhabited and were used to establish colonies or military installations, while others belonged to civilizations subjugated by Klingon invasion. Despite its reputation for ruthlessness, the Klingon Empire and the worlds that it comprises are very carefully overseen. It has been more than two centuries since a conquered world or system has attempted to resist imperial governance, as most of these societies see the benefit of continued association with their rulers. As a result, each of these planets has their own set of Klingon-centric holidays and other cultural observances. Access to these regions is subject to change depending on the time of year, so plan accordingly!

USING THIS GUIDE

Many of the names for commercial establishments featured in this guide are rendered in native *pIqaD*, or "Klingonese," although a few of the merchants contacted for inclusion in this guide grudgingly agreed to provide appropriate translations or their own tourist-friendly alternatives. However, don't expect Klingon signage to be accommodating to offworlders who don't speak the lingo. If you can't decipher the signs when searching for a specific location, you can always consult a visitor assistance center or simply access the planet's global positioning satellite network.

TIPS FOR A FUN TRIP

• Here's a secret: Qo'noS is beautiful, especially once you get away from the cities. Though it has suffered over generations from overpopulation, resource shortages, and natural calamity, significant portions of the planet harbor a breathtaking beauty that rivals anything you might find elsewhere in the quadrant. Whatever you do, make sure you take time for at least one overnight excursion away from the cities and into the wilderness. Sleep under the stars in the foothills surrounding the Lake of Lusor or in the boundless forests of the Ketha Lowlands. On clear nights in these areas, larger fragments from the Praxis asteroid belt are visible to the naked eye, and pieces of the destroyed moon occasionally make planet fall.

• Unless you are traversing areas that are accessible only via air or water vehicles, travel over land whenever possible and appropriate. While shuttles and transporters are available in the First City and other major population centers, don't bypass a chance to behold the planet's natural and often harsh beauty from as close a vantage point as possible. Magnetic-rail transports connect most major destinations, with plenty of landmarks and other points of interest to see along the way, but if you've got the time, opt for the historic rail lines, which still utilize wheeled trains powered by gas turbines. Constructed centuries ago using conscripted labor from subjugated worlds, these rail lines are preserved in order to connect travelers to a network of historic sites such as battlefields, shrines, village remnants, and natural formations. These include Kri'stak Volcano and Kang's Summit, which aren't accessible on the more modern, direct routes. Despite their age, the rail lines are kept in prime working order, in defiance of repeated calls to replace them with modern technology.

• Due to the tilt of its axis, Qo'noS is routinely subjected to a broad spectrum of weather and climate extremes. Add to this the high levels of constant volcanic activity and the effects of prolonged industrialization, and don't be surprised if you find yourself dealing with massive storms or sudden, severe shifts in temperature. Those touring the planet without benefit of a group or guide should check ahead at any destination and be prepared for weather delays and cancellations.

• Though Qo'noS is Class M and therefore capable of supporting most humanoid life-forms, the high concentrations of methane and other pollutants may make breathing difficult for certain species. Despite decades of terraforming to reduce the levels of atmospheric contamination, some areas of the planet will be either deemed off-limits, or only accessible through the use of environmental suits or other breathing equipment. Travelers with respiratory ailments are strongly urged to avoid these regions.

WHAT TO WEAR

Qo'noS experiences a wide range of weather, with the planet's landmass, or "supercontinent," spanning multiple climate zones. However, conditions in the major population centers and main points of tourist interest tend toward the mild to warm side. Travelers seeking adventure away from these areas should be prepared to deal with sudden weather changes. Dress or be ready to replicate clothing that's appropriate for a variety of situations, especially when considering outdoor activities. Durable, comfortable footwear suitable for prolonged walking and leisure hiking is a must. Conservative dress is encouraged in the outlying areas that have not yet adapted to the more cosmopolitan attitudes of the larger cities. When you are hiking in the jungles, bright-colored clothing may prove useful if you become lost or separated from your tour group. On the other hand, bright colors also tend to attract large predators such as saber bears and brush devils. The basic rule of thumb is "dress for dinner, not as dinner."

With respect to local fashion or style, Klingons generally don't subscribe to fads or trends. Most people associate Klingon fashion with military uniforms and accessories, and it's true that soldiers of the Empire do treat their attire with particular reverence. While civilian clothing worn for work or other day-to-day activities tends toward utilitarian garments designed with durability and protection in mind, Klingons spare no effort when it comes to dressing for formal occasions of every stripe. Handcrafted from leather, silk, and other fabrics, vibrantly colored gowns and robes that accentuate the unique Klingon physiology are a common sight.

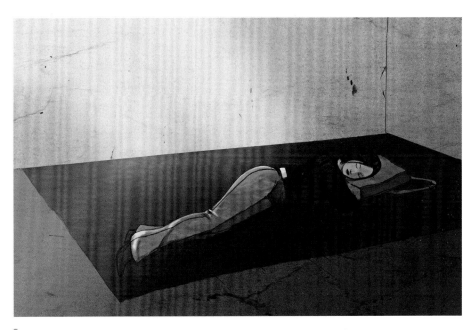

🛏 LODGING TIPS

You'll find a broad assortment of guest lodging options, especially in the larger cities, from hotels and cottages established with offworlders in mind, to gatehouse-type quarters or camping areas, and other venues with varying levels of comfort that carry a more traditional local appeal. Klingons take pride in not pampering themselves, even while sleeping, so, when staying outside major cities, be prepared to recline on hard, flat rock, or metal surfaces. In contrast, Quin'lat, Krennla, and the First City in particular offer more welcoming accommodations for numerous species from throughout the Beta and Alpha Quadrants. Just don't expect the sort of options you'd find at a more typical Federation vacation destination. When venturing away from the major population centers to the Ketha Lowlands or the Central Plains for any extended period, consider including a comfortable sleeping bag or other bedding with your luggage. Some merchants in these areas will sell or rent these items, but be forewarned that the selection will vary from place to place.

 With the exception of those hotels operated in the larger cities by offworlders, Klingon accommodations tend to be staffed by natives rather than the wide array of species you might find working in hotels on other planets such as Vulcan or Andor. Reservations for scheduled tour groups are almost always honored, but accommodating Klingon travelers will always take precedence over catering to offworlders traveling independently. This is most definitely the case in smaller towns and remote provinces. Klingon merchants and proprietors tend to be brusque if not outright rude, and most interactions with them and their staff will be short and to the point.

ETIQUETTE

The concept of honor is irrevocably woven into every facet of Klingon culture. It's a keystone of their civilization, dating back to the time of Kahless the Unforgettable. According to history and mythology, Kahless all but single-handedly forged what would become the Klingon Empire,

founding it upon the principles of honor and duty, with a warrior ethos that persists to this day. The name Kahless is spoken with reverence across the planet, from the lowliest soldier to the leaders of every Great House and family.

Though visitors are becoming more welcome on Qo'noS, especially in the larger population centers, travelers may still encounter some wariness toward offworlders, especially from older Klingons and in those regions that are less traveled. When traveling, bear in mind that, with few exceptions, Klingons value adherence to tradition and a wide range of ceremonial rituals. Many of these customs have become familiar to offworlders thanks to centuries of contact between Klingons and other species, but some practices remain closely guarded from outside eyes.

Failing to acknowledge or respect a particular observance can be considered a grievous insult not just to an individual but even that person's entire family and—depending on the specific offense—Klingon society as a whole. In extreme cases, it's entirely possible for wayward travelers to find themselves inadvertently challenged to a fight simply because they have spoken in too soft a voice or stood too far away while conversing.

Patient and inquisitive travelers with a genuine desire to learn will find that many Klingons are more than willing to impart knowledge on these topics. If you get the chance, enjoy a meal with locals and share in the fellowship that comes from such gatherings. You will hear stories. You will sing songs, and you will celebrate all that it means to be Klingon. Many locals, especially in more rural areas, tend to be late-night revelers. Be ready to listen to off-key renditions of various drinking songs that last into the wee hours. There will also be fighting, as no Klingon drinking establishment can be considered respectable without a good brawl breaking out at least once a night. There may even be the occasional duel to the death, so don't be surprised to see *d'k tahg* knife play breaking out in the streets when a challenge is made.

AUTHOR'S NOTE:

Various flavors of bloodwine are a perennial favorite of many Klingons but might be too potent for some offworlders. On the other hand, *warnog* beer and a number of ales might be more to your liking. Please drink responsibly.

DID YOU KNOW?

SAYING "HELLO" AND "GOOD-BYE" ON QO'NOS

It's true that *tlhIngan Hol,* just one of many varieties of spoken language that fall under the label "Klingonese," is difficult to learn, and offworlders can spend years becoming proficient. Mastery is a matter of some debate, particularly when considering the hundreds of dialect variations that have been recorded over the course of Klingon history. While most outsiders tend to rely on universal translators to cover the language gap, Klingons will usually appreciate sincere efforts to communicate using their native tongue. Travelers can often make do with a few key terms and phrases and a little practice.

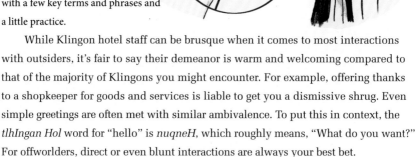

While Klingon hotel staff can be brusque when it comes to most interactions with outsiders, it's fair to say their demeanor is warm and welcoming compared to that of the majority of Klingons you might encounter. For example, offering thanks to a shopkeeper for goods and services is liable to get you a dismissive shrug. Even simple greetings are often met with similar ambivalence. To put this in context, the *tlhIngan Hol* word for "hello" is *nuqneH*, which roughly means, "What do you want?" For offworlders, direct or even blunt interactions are always your best bet.

On the other hand, Klingons can be quite energetic when exchanging greetings with one another. For males in particular, it's not unusual to see them hitting each other on the arms or even exchanging hearty embraces. If they've been drinking, don't be surprised to see a headbutt or two. This isn't any sort of formally recognized greeting, of course, but it's still quite the sight when two lumbering, inebriated warriors address one another in this fashion.

Unless your skull is a strong as a Klingon's, we advise against engaging in such salutations.

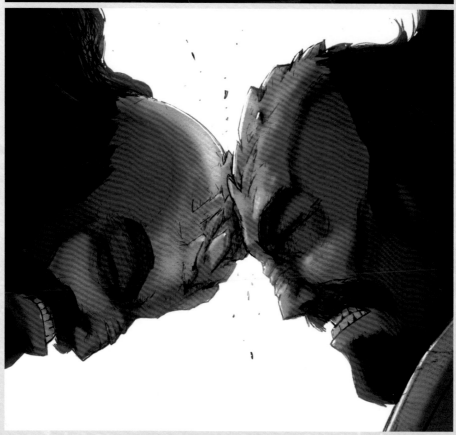

THE KLINGON EMPIRE
A BRIEF HISTORY FOR VISITORS

Couched in mystery and legend, the origins of the Klingon Empire are a matter of much debate among historians and other scholars, let alone any son or daughter born on Qo'noS. According to ancient folklore, the planet was once visited by aliens possessing technology and abilities that made them gods in the eyes of the native Klingons. These beings enslaved the indigenous people but eventually were vanquished when Klingon resistance fighters took up arms and slew their oppressors. Such tales eventually gave rise to the popular claim that the Klingons killed all of their gods before seizing their own destiny.

EARLY HISTORY, EARLY CHAOS

The planet's early history is one of rampant war that all but consumed numerous Klingon tribes. Such conflicts were driven by territory and resource control, religious disputes, or simple survival in the face of oppression or annihilation. Entire cities and their populations were wiped from existence merely because they happened to be caught in the crossfire of two warring factions. Molor, a brutal tyrant who ruled over the largest faction of Klingon civilization, was the planet's de facto ruler, directing his armies against anyone who might dare stand against him. Historians believe that Molor's bloodlust for conflict and conquest drove Klingon civilization to the very precipice of self-destruction. It was during this period, which some historians would later refer to as the Heroic Age of Qo'noS, that leaders and visionaries began to emerge from the smoke of battle. Such figures attracted increasing numbers of followers as they strived to throw off Molor's reign of violence and terror and unite Klingons as one people. In the early days of their emergence, these outspoken individuals, along with their supporters, were killed for daring to express such unconventional ideas.

THE RISE OF KAHLESS THE UNFORGETTABLE

In the midst of ever-escalating warfare that threatened all of Klingon civilization, there emerged an extraordinary warrior: Kahless. Already known among military and political leaders for his tactical prowess, he began speaking out against the status quo, directly challenging Molor's authority. Modifying spiritual lessons taught to him by clerics during childhood, he encouraged his soldiers to abandon the wanton selfishness and savagery that had characterized warfare between the various tribes scattered around the planet for generations. Instead, Kahless inspired his followers to cultivate a true "warrior ethos" while embracing the values of personal and ancestral honor. War, he contended, must be waged for constructive purpose and conducted in a manner befitting a superior species. That meant respect even for vanquished enemies, who, even while living under imperial rule, still contributed to the continued success and expansion of Klingon influence.

As Molor continued his campaign to crush potential enemies and the other tribes continued to fight one another, the teachings of Kahless began to take hold. His military audacity was matched only by an unwavering dedication to molding the outlook of not just the military but all of the Klingon people. As his battlefield triumphs began to mount, so too did Kahless's sway over the civilian populace, who saw him not just as a military commander but also a desirable successor to Molor and leader for all Klingons. Kahless scored victory after victory as he pushed back against the tyrant's rule, until the two leaders finally met face-to-face at the River Skral in what is now known as the Ketha Lowlands. After hours of savage combat, Kahless slew Molor with a bladed weapon he had forged with his own hands—the first *bat'leth*. In the wake of this triumph, Kahless ascended to the deceased tyrant's throne, and Molor's former subjects welcomed this change of regime. A benevolent victor, Kahless was able to convince former enemies to join him, ultimately uniting all of the warring tribes under one flag. Now a single force under the rule of Emperor Kahless, the Klingon Empire soon extended its influence across the planet, eventually bonding all the people of Qo'noS.

Kahless is credited with pulling back the Klingon people from the brink of oblivion and establishing a code of honor that continues to drive the entire civilization to this day. Indeed, as centuries passed, the truth of Kahless's actual accomplishments began to be eclipsed by tales of monumental feats well beyond the abilities of a mere mortal—popular myths about Kahless see him single-handedly triumphing over an entire rival army at Three Turn Bridge and battling against supernatural adversaries seeking to destroy his Empire. As a result, the legend of Kahless has become a cornerstone of Klingon mythology as well as history.

DID YOU KNOW?
THE SYMBOL OF THE KLINGON EMPIRE

Klingons call it *tlq ghob*, which translates roughly to "the Heart of Virtue." The mark of the Empire traces its roots back to the time of Kahless and the three-bladed weapon that the legendary warrior preferred to carry into battle. He adopted a stylized representation of the weapon to serve as the symbol of his family, the House of Kahless, and that icon soon became synonymous with the Empire itself.

The Heart of Virtue's three blades represent a balance between three bedrock character traits of the Klingon people: honor, loyalty, and duty. As Kahless once noted, none of these things can exist without the others. This philosophy is drilled into every young Klingon military-academy cadet.

EXPANSION AND CONQUEST

After being united by Kahless, the Empire turned its attention to sowing fear into the hearts of enemies who might lurk beyond the confines of their own world. After developing interstellar faster-than-light propulsion to carry their warships, the Empire began spreading outward from Qo'noS. This resulted in the Klingons encountering a more advanced race, the Hur'q, who in turn invaded and captured the Klingon homeworld world during the fourteenth century (as measured on the Gregorian calendar). After generations under Hur'q rule, the Klingon people rallied and evicted their oppressors, but not before Qo'noS was left in near ruin.

With the planet's plentiful natural resources plundered and many of its significant cultural artifacts stolen or destroyed, the Empire vowed it would never again bow before an enemy. Colonies were established on over a dozen planets, extending the Klingon influence ever farther as other worlds and their populations were brought under imperial rule. But even as the Empire continued to grow, there were other interstellar powers that would not yield quite so easily.

CONTACT WITH EARTH AND THE FEDERATION

When a Klingon scout craft accidentally crashed on Earth in the mid-twenty-second century, the Empire became aware of humans for the first time. It was a rocky beginning to a hostile relationship, with tensions and skirmishes escalating to the point of war on multiple occasions. The situation was not helped when, in 2154, the Empire attempted to develop genetically enhanced "super soldiers," basing their efforts on successful attempts by humans to create similar forces. During the experiments, Klingon scientists tried to modify their race's DNA using genetically engineered human embryos as a starting point, but the first attempts resulted in Klingon genetic code being overwritten by the aggressive, adaptable human genes.

A more immediate side effect emerged when the augmented DNA of one test subject combined with a potent strain of Levodian flu, resulting in what became known as the "Qu'Vat virus." This new contagion spread at an alarming rate, its notable symptom being the physical mutation of exposed Klingons. The most obvious aspect of this change was the loss of the prominent cranial ridges, giving those afflicted a more human appearance—a fate many Klingons found objectionable and embarrassing. The often deadly infection continued to spread and threatened to wipe out the Klingon race. Though the genetic experiments were halted and a cure was found for Qu'Vat, the physiological effects, including the loss of the cranial ridges, were permanent. Those affected were labeled QuchHa', or "the unhappy ones," and these genetic mutations were also passed to their offspring. The disease and its effects were most pronounced throughout the remaining years of the twenty-second century and into the early and mid-2200s.

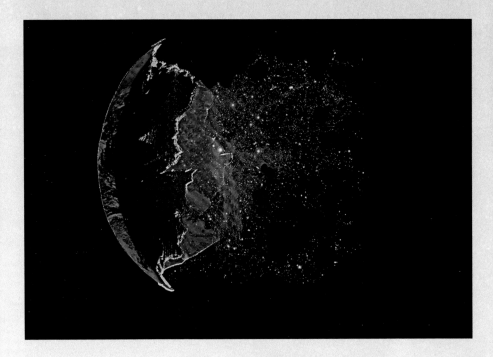

Relations between the Empire and the Federation remained tense for more than a century before the Empire declared open war on its rival in 2267. However, that campaign was stopped short by a race of omnipotent super beings, the Organians, who imposed their will upon both parties and thereby stifled Klingon efforts to conquer the humans and their allies. This Organian Peace Treaty established the Neutral Zone between Klingon and Federation space, and forbade outright hostilities within that region. Although occasional, limited skirmishes still occurred elsewhere, both imperial and Federation leaders agreed to adhere to the spirit of the treaty and avoid open hostilities. Following the imposition of this agreement, the Organians were not heard from for many years, prompting some members of the Klingon High Council to call for war in their absence. Such appeals were largely ignored by the Council's more pragmatic voices.

Despite condemning the audacity of humans and their propensity for inserting themselves into the affairs of others, some Klingon warriors and governmental leaders would come to admire their guile. This grudging respect, more so than any isolated confrontation or diplomatic overture, would play a large role in the eventual warming of Klingon-Federation relations. This budding friendship was underscored in 2293, when the explosion of Praxis, a moon orbiting Qo'noS, wreaked havoc on the planet's atmosphere and prompted the Klingon government to reach out to the Federation for emergency assistance. This remarkable act of trust on both sides would prove to be a turning point in the history of both peoples.

THE EMPIRE TODAY

Following the reign of Kahless, successive emperors continued to rule over the Klingon people for centuries. However, as the Empire expanded its influence across the planet, authority was increasingly assigned to delegates in different regions. Most of these initial delegates were the heads of prominent Klingon families, giving rise to the "Great Houses," the patriarchs of which became members of the first Klingon High Council. Over time, the role of emperor was seen as unnecessary, and in the mid-twenty-first century, the emperor was replaced by a chancellor charged with presiding over the Council. It was during this period that most historians agree modern Klingon civilization emerged, with some calling it the Birth of the Second Klingon Empire.

Despite this progress, the Klingon people continued to endure unrest into the twenty-fourth century. Civil war raged on Qo'noS and other imperial worlds, and there were conflicts with numerous interstellar powers, including the Cardassian Union and the Romulan Empire. Even the fragile peace enjoyed with the Federation faltered during the first decades of the new century, resulting in a number of clashes between Klingon and Starfleet warships, which brought with them the renewed prospect of all-out war. Confronting all of these demands placed a heavy strain on the Empire's overextended military and its ever-decreasing pool of resources. As neighboring rivals expanded their borders, the Empire was in danger of being trapped with no avenues for growth.

Perhaps the most significant moment in recent Klingon history came in 2369, with the apparent reappearance of Kahless. In accordance with legend and his own promise, the first emperor did indeed seem to return to this life, appearing on the planet Boreth. However, it was soon learned that clerics there had in fact created a clone of the emperor with DNA reportedly taken from the original Kahless's blood. The clerics had developed the clone in the hopes that the Klingon people would look to him for leadership and this newfound unity would heal the wounds that had threatened to doom the Empire. Gowron, who had only recently assumed his role as  Chancellor of the Klingon High Council, was eventually convinced to reinstate the role of emperor, making Kahless's clone a ceremonial figurehead of the Klingon government. In accordance with the legendary warrior's own predictions from centuries ago, Kahless—or his clone at least—once again stood as a symbol of the Empire's former greatness and an exemplar of Klingon honor.

The pressures brought by tensions with political rivals were all but forgotten in 2373, when the Empire and the Federation found themselves in conflict with the Dominion, an interstellar consortium located in the distant Gamma Quadrant. Ruled by a race of shape changers known as "the Founders," the Dominion and its legions of genetically engineered soldiers, the Jem'Hadar, launched an invasion against the Federation with designs on conquering the entire Alpha Quadrant. Seeing the need for an alliance to defeat this common foe, the Klingon Empire elected to stand with the Federation and fight back against the Dominion. It was this collaboration that forever sealed the bond between the Empire and the Federation. While it remains troubled at times, it is an alliance that continues to this day.

tlhIngan Hol! DO YOU SPEAK IT?

A KLINGON LANGUAGE PRIMER

Klingons take their native tongue seriously, as they do many other aspects of their culture. Likewise, *tlhIngan Hol*, or "Klingonese," is a robust and multifaceted language that embodies many of the same qualities that define those who speak it.

As such, don't forget to pack your universal translator. Though Federation Standard is spoken on Qo'noS in many of the major metropolitan centers, some locals will refuse to speak it. Unless you've actually taken extensive courses in speaking the local languages, we strongly recommend relying on your translator so as not to unwittingly cause offence. However, if you do feel the need to have a few key phrases memorized, we suggest learning and practicing the following:

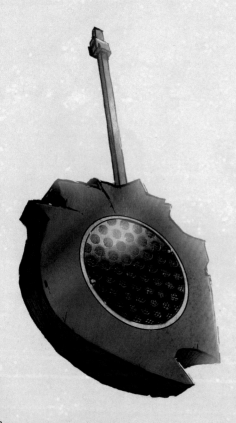

'arlogh Qoylu'pu'? – What time is it?

bortaS bIr jablu'DI' reH QaQqu' nay'. – Revenge is a dish best served cold.

Heghlu'meH QaQ jajvam. – Today is a good day to die.

jIQoS. – I am sorry.

meQtaHbogh qachDaq Suv qoH neH. – Only a fool fights in a burning house.

nuqDaq 'oH puchpa''e'? – Where is the bathroom?

nuqDaq 'oH Qe' QaQ? – Where is a good restaurant?

nuqneH. – Hello; also, What do you want?

Qapla'! – Success!

qatlho'. – Thank you. (Remember, many Klingons usually ignore such platitudes.)

Many Klingon terms don't translate directly to Federation Standard, so expect to hear these common terms and phrases throughout your visit:

Bat'leth: "Sword of Honor." A favored bladed weapon of many a Klingon warrior, this large, curved blade takes years to master and has been a key component of Klingon culture dating back thousands of years, when legends say that Kahless the Unforgettable forged the first *bat'leth*. You won't find these weapons in retail shops, as most Klingons refuse to sell any representations of this sacred weapon to offworlders.

D'k tahg: Another favored weapon, this is a smaller dagger normally worn on the belt of a Klingon's military uniform or concealed in a boot or beneath civilian clothing. The knife's identifying characteristic is its double-edged blade offset by a pair of smaller, hinged blades that spring from the dagger's handle. Like the *bat'leth*, the *d'k tahg* holds great ceremonial value in Klingon culture and is often the weapon of choice for settling disputes that escalate to personal combat. To steal a warrior's *d'k tahg* is to insult his honor.

Fek'lhr: The Klingon equivalent of Satan, Apophis, or Mephistopheles, and guardian of the underworld of *Gre'thor*.

Gik'tal: "To the death." You're going to hear this one a lot.

Gre'thor: The Klingon equivalent of Naraka, Gehenna, or Hell.

'Iw bIQtIq: In Klingon mythology, "the River of Blood." Legends say that Klingon warriors who have died honorably in battle are able to cross the river so that they might join the Black Fleet in *Sto-Vo-Kor*, the Klingon afterlife.

Klin zha: A popular strategy board game, on par with chess or *Terrace*, or the Romulan game *latrunclo*. Like those games, *Klin zha* requires quick thinking as well as the ability to plan and execute long-form strategic positioning while denying those same advantages to one's opponent. *Klin zha* tournaments are frequently held throughout the Empire, and the game has also achieved modest popularity among Starfleet personnel and in gaming parlors and casinos on various resort planets.

Mauk-to'Vor: A ceremonial ritual in which a disgraced Klingon warrior with no hope of regaining honor in this life asks a sibling to end their life. The shamed Klingon requests the ceremony in order to have their honor restored and thereby earn the right to be sent to *Sto-Vo-Kor* (see below).

Nentay: Rite of Ascension. A two-part coming-of-age ceremony in which a young Klingon is officially recognized as a warrior.

Ql'tu': In Klingon mythology, paradise, or the source from which all life on Qo'noS sprang.

QuchHa': The unhappy ones. Specifically, this term refers to those Klingons who were affected in the twenty-second century by the Qu'Vat virus, either directly or as a result of heredity. The main consequence of the virus was to rob the infected Klingons of their prominent cranial ridges. It also undermined or impeded their overall physiology so that they more closely resembled humans. *QuchHa'* have all but died off, but you may well encounter the odd specimen during your travels.

R'uustai: A ceremony in which two individuals who are not linked by blood or marriage are bonded together, making them siblings and members of each other's houses and families.

Sto-Vo-Kor: This is the afterlife sought by all Klingon warriors, comparable to Elysium from Greek mythology. It is here that those deemed worthy are accepted into everlasting service to the Empire, destined to fight an unending battle against great adversaries.

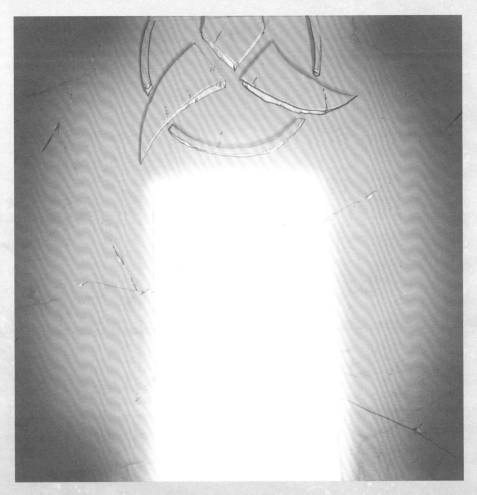

THE FIRST CITY

KANNAG

'IWLIJ JACHJAJ
NIGHTCLUB

SORIDIEM'S
KLIN ZHA
PARLOR

HAPWIJ NAGH MEBPA'MEY
(FLAT ROCK HOTEL)

VEB QUARTER

WEJDICH QUARTER

FEDERATION
EMBASSY

THE FII

RIVERFRONT
ENCLAVE

KAHLESS
MUSEUM

QAM-CH

UNTAINS

CAVES OF
NO'MAT

N

KIRETEK'S
INN

THE GREAT HALL

VOTAQ'S

HOTEL
JARANTINE

OLD QUARTER

RECLAW MUSEUM

QAV QUARTER

HAN'VRAL
AMPHITHEATER

PAO'LA OPEN
AIR BAZAAR

HALL OF
WARRIORS

ST CITY

ORDER OF THE
BAT'LETH SHRINE

HALL OF
HONOR

RIVER

SHOPPING &
RECREATION

DINING &
NIGHTLIFE

LODGING

LOOKING TO EXPERIENCE ALL OF QO'NOS in one handy package? You can't do any better than a trip to the sprawling, storied metropolis that is the First City, or *veng wa'Dich*, as the locals call it. Not just the planet's capital, it's also the seat of power for all of the Klingon Empire.

Located near the western edge of the planet's major continental landmass, the First City sits along the Qam-Chee River. In ancient times, the river facilitated commerce and trade as well as the movement of military forces to the Sea of Gatan and westward to the PoSbIQ'a' Ocean. Originally a fortress set within the protective boundaries of a mountain range, the First City predates even the Age of Kahless. As Kahless's influence continued to expand along with that of the budding Klingon Empire, the one-time stronghold was chosen to serve as the center of imperial power. The city that sprang up around the fortress would continue to grow during the ensuing years, eventually becoming the major metropolis it is today.

The First City is a visual delight for travelers looking to immerse themselves in the history and culture of a civilization as long-lived as the Klingon Empire. It is an amalgam of ancient and modern architectural styles spanning centuries of enduring and defunct dynasties and Great Houses. The oldest structures bear testimony to the city's origins as a military fortress, with designs reflecting the necessity for defense against aerial assaults. Though constructed for martial purposes, these buildings still harbor a majestic beauty that must be experienced firsthand in order to be fully appreciated.

Offworlders live and work within the city's boundaries, many of them diplomatic workers assigned to a variety of embassies located in the capital. There is also a large population of non-Klingon permanent residents, primarily beings from worlds that have recently become Klingon allies, along with the descendants of species subjugated by the Empire who later came to appreciate Klingon rule. The First City is also home to many merchants who hail from a wide range of races and planets. Tellarites in particular seem to find the city agreeable, and many natives attribute this to their Klingon-like temperament. While humans, Vulcans, and other prominent Federation-member worlds are represented thanks to the aforementioned embassy staffs or Starfleet contingents, you won't find many Cardassians due to ongoing disputes between their people and the Klingon Empire. It's also very unlikely you'll see any Romulans, despite the very shaky truce their empire enjoys with the Klingons. Even Ferengi, who rarely pass up promising business ventures, have yet to fully embrace the opportunities that come with the growing tourism industry on Qo'noS. Unlike other planets, such as Vulcan, where outsiders have been permitted to build homes and businesses that retain some architectural connection to their own home worlds, the First City allows no such opportunities and retains its unshakable regal aesthetic.

 ## GETTING AROUND

The city is divided into quarters, each of which was built independently from the others during different major periods of Klingon history. The Old Quarter, for example, contains the remains of the original settlements that sprang up in the shadow of the fortress that predates the city. Public transportation is abundant, though you'll get the most from your visit by walking the streets that connect the historic districts with the more modern lodging, dining, and entertainment venues. It's during such wandering that you'll be able to experience aspects of Klingon culture less familiar to offworlders. You'll find small cathedrals that have stood for hundreds of years, along with art galleries and libraries that celebrate the Empire's past and present. Many of the city's citizens, particularly on the outskirts, tend to their own gardens and greenhouses, so don't be surprised if you're offered a fresh *pe'bot* or some other specimen of succulent Klingon fruit or vegetable.

THE FIRST CITY: ALL THAT IS KLINGON

[First published in the 2379 Edition]
I carry the distinction of being the first Klingon to serve as a commissioned officer of the Federation Starfleet. Because of this and the experiences of my childhood, I like to think that I possess a unique perspective on both Klingon and Federation societies. Though I have spent the majority of my life away from Qo'noS, it is the planet of my birth and the world I call my true home. Despite all of this, it was only as an adult that I finally journeyed to the First City. I recall the awe I experienced as I beheld the Great Hall, and the sensation that Kahless himself was looking down upon me and welcoming me into the true birthplace of the Klingon Empire.

I sometimes wonder what my life would be like if my parents had not elected to take me to live on the Khitomer colony outpost. What might have happened if they had not perished during an attack by Romulan forces? I likely would have died as a result of that attack if I had not been found by Sergey Rozhenko, a benevolent human serving aboard the Starfleet vessel *U.S.S. Intrepid*. What path might I have traveled if Sergey and his wife, Helena, had not chosen to raise me alongside their own son, Nikolai, on the planet Gault?

There are those who think my youth was wasted, living as I was on a Federation farming colony. Those people are wrong. As an outsider from a very young age and seemingly forgotten by my own people, I was forced to find my place among those who were viewed as enemies of the Empire. As an adolescent, I endeavored to maintain a tangible connection to my Klingon heritage. I undertook the Rite of Ascension, intending to become a warrior in service to the Empire. However, it was while meditating in the Caves of No'Mat that I was visited by a vision of the Emperor Kahless, who told me I would go on to do something no Klingon had ever done. I do not know if he meant joining Starfleet, but I like to think so.

While my Starfleet career has been most satisfying, it has not lessened my dedication to the Klingon people. It was because of my appointment as the Federation's ambassador to the Empire that I came to truly know and appreciate the First City and its heritage. I have walked these streets, speaking with the people who live here and immersing myself in the history they safeguard, and that has only served to deepen my bond with my home planet. For a time, I considered remaining here, and perhaps ascending to a seat on the High Council, before deciding that I could be of greater use elsewhere.

The honor is to serve, and if my destiny is to serve as a bridge between the Empire and the Federation, then it is a legacy I am proud to bear.

—Commander Worf, *U.S.S. Enterprise*

◉ SIGHTS AND ACTIVITIES

Despite the influx of offworlders in recent decades, the First City remains
undeniably Klingon, and its distinguished history is etched into its every edifice.
Centuries of war, strife, and even occupation by another conquering race
have all failed to wipe away the ancestry enshrined here. Ancient architecture
stands alongside modern infrastructure, all connected by an intricate network
of timeworn stone streets and walking paths, as well as modern mag-rail lines
and even the Qam-Chee River, which can be traversed by boat. Speaking of the
river, there are those who believe it harbors a portal to *Gre'thor*, the Klingon
underworld, where the Barge of the Dead ferries lost souls to eternal damnation. If
you choose a riverboat as a means of getting around the city, don't be surprised if
your pilot regales you with such a story.

▲ The Great Hall

Located near the center of the Old Quarter and housed within the original
fortress that served as the seed from which the First City grew, the Great Hall
is the figurative and literal heart of the Klingon Empire. The centerpiece of the
hall is the immense chamber in which the High Council meets to deliberate
issues of the day. Most proceedings are open to the public, with the exception
of those pertaining to security or other sensitive matters, so don't be surprised
to see Klingon civilians alongside offworld travelers following the debates from
the observer's galleries. The hall also contains a statue of Kahless, as well as an
extensive exhibit highlighting his indelible role in Klingon history. Children of all
ages are invited to visit the exhibit's learning center, where they will be treated to
a performance by a Kahless impersonator entertaining audiences with tales of the
legendary emperor's more outlandish exploits.

▲ Hall of Warriors

Situated in the city's southeast quarter and overlooking the Qam-Chee River, the
Hall of Warriors is one of the most revered locations on the planet, rivaling even
the Great Hall itself. Enshrined here are statues showcasing notable Klingons
who've distinguished themselves in a manner that exceeds even the exacting
demands placed upon soldiers of the Empire. Originally conceived as a military
memorial, the Hall has benefited from the recent addition of a wing devoted to
civilians and even a few offworlders recognized for their significant contributions
to the Klingon people. Prominent inductees here include Jean-Luc Picard, the
famed Starfleet captain who holds the distinction of being the only non-Klingon
ever to preside over the appointment of a new Chancellor of the High Council.
Enshrinement in the Hall guarantees eternal respect from all Klingons until the
end of time. Although the Hall carries no retail outlets, literature and holovisual
documentary materials highlighting the various heroes can be found in nearby
merchant shops.

DID YOU KNOW?

THE GREAT TRIBBLE HUNT

Klingon history is replete with engrossing
tales of glorious combat, including acts
of courage and daring by noble warriors
who have fought and died in service to the
Empire. From the ancient wars that form
the bedrock of Klingon society to more recent
conflicts with the Romulans, the Cardassian
Union, and the Dominion, many a great battle is
passionately celebrated in story and song.

Except one.

Klingons don't deny that such a campaign was ever waged, but they also don't
go out of their way to acknowledge the bizarre crusade undertaken against the species
Polygeminus grex, the small, seemingly harmless life-forms known throughout the
quadrant by their common name, "tribbles." Genetically primed for reproduction, these
little, furry organisms seem to exist for one purpose: to multiply. The consumption of
any food source accelerates a tribble's pregnancy to alarming degrees, with but a single
specimen capable of producing scores of offspring within hours. While humans and other
life-forms tend to fawn over the creatures, Klingons had come to view tribbles as nothing
more than a direct threat to the security of the Empire by the mid-twenty-third century.

Klingons came to know of these life-forms thanks to the untimely visit of the warship
IKS Gr'oth to a Federation deep space station. The tribbles were already on their way to
taking over the outpost, multiplying and spreading like a disease. Having made their way
aboard a Starfleet battle cruiser, the *U.S.S. Enterprise*, they soon infiltrated the *Gr'oth* and
multiplied to the point that they all but buried the ship's crew.

Humiliated in the eyes of his fellow Klingons, the *Gr'oth's* captain, Koloth, vowed
not to rest until every tribble was destroyed. Leading a Klingon armada across space,
Koloth tracked the tribbles from planet to planet, eradicating them at every turn until
finally discovering the location of their home world, which he did not hesitate to
obliterate.

And yet, tribbles survive.

No one knows for sure how any of them managed to escape total annihilation, but
there's no denying their continued existence. Rumors persist that a small number of the
creatures were brought through time from a point in the past, prior to their supposed
eradication. A more likely explanation is that some simply survived the Great Tribble
Hunt and lived to breed another day.

Though no tribbles are allowed on Qo'noS, curious visitors can still learn about
them and the Empire's campaign against them thanks to an exhibit at the Hall of Warriors
devoted to the life and achievements of Captain Koloth.

▼ Federation Embassy

At first glance, it's easy to mistake this massive, inverted pyramidal structure as one of several ancient relics maintained for historical value rather than what it is: an institution indicative of the more progressive nature of modern Klingon society. At one time a military garrison headquarters for legions of Kahless's imperial guard, this eye-catching structure located southwest of the Great Hall in the *wejDIch* Quarter is the home of Federation authority on Qo'noS. Surrounded by a force-field barrier as well as a physical fence standing ten meters high, the embassy is sovereign Federation soil, and it's here that Federation citizens with travel issues or other concerns can come for assistance. The embassy also contains a museum dedicated to the long, often tumultuous relationship between the Empire and the Federation. Included in the exhibit is a holographic re-creation of the 2372 invasion of the embassy by Klingon forces, which occurred when the Empire temporarily withdrew from its peace agreement with the Federation following a dispute with the Cardassian Union. Visitors will find artifacts, documents, and presentations highlighting the two powers' joint history.

▲ The Old Quarter

As the name indicates, this is the oldest part of the First City, located in its northeastern quadrant. It grew out of the first primitive settlements as Klingons from across the planet migrated here in the earliest days of the Empire under Kahless's rule. During the first emperor's reign, as he struggled to solidify his power base, frequent assaults on the city by ragtag armies—remnants of forces who once were loyal to Molor and who later fled to the outlying territories where they continued to act as marauders—forced the hasty construction of ever greater defenses. This spawned more settlements as increasing numbers of migrating Klingons arrived, seeking protection in the fortified city. Many of these new settlers had fled the oppressive rule of other tribal leaders, while others were looking for a new start after Kahless defeated their overlords' forces in battle. The Old Quarter grew out of those original, disparate communities, evolving from simple military fortifications into a thriving city. These days, walking tours guide visitors through the remnants of the first villages that sprang up around the original fortress constructed here, and costumed performers entertain and inform visitors about the history of the burgeoning region. Traversing the web of side streets and walking paths, bridges and tunnels that connect the Quarter's main thoroughfares to the rest of the city allow visitors to sample a variety of retail shops, galleries, museums, and historical landmarks.

▼ Order of the *Bat'leth* Shrine

Located adjacent to the Hall of Warriors along the Qam-Chee River, this memorial is small enough that it can easily be added to any excursion to this part of the First City. The site combines a monument, museum, and archive, which together provide visitors with insight into the Order of the *Bat'leth*—the most celebrated award that a Klingon warrior can receive. Created in the ninth century by Lady Lukara, widow to Emperor Kahless, the Order serves as a constant reminder that all Klingons should continually strive to meet the standard exemplified by her husband. Entry into the Order symbolizes the highest standards of personal honor, courage, and accomplishment in battle. The shrine's museum chronicles the group's history, enhanced by displays featuring artifacts, weapons, and other personal items spanning centuries of superlative service to the Klingon Empire by some of its most cherished warriors.

Kahless Historical Museum

Though there are many museums, galleries, and monuments dedicated to the life and accomplishments of Kahless the Unforgettable, this is the only archive that has existed since the time of his rule. The museum's curators have been able to chronicle his career and accomplishments beginning with his first days as emperor through to his death. Many of these records were lost during the Hur'q occupation of Qo'noS, but in the centuries since, archaeologists and historians have traveled the planet seeking to rebuild this unique repository. Although the museum was originally an annex to the Great Hall, the sheer number of retrieved items, along with the need for dedicated conservation and restoration efforts, demanded a larger dedicated space. The result is this larger building located in the southwestern or *wejDIch* Quarter. Here, visitors are able to view an impressive collection of artifacts, including numerous items once possessed by Kahless and his immediate family.

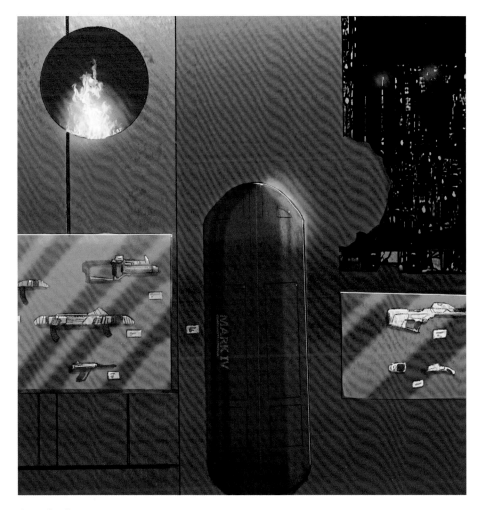

▲ Hall of Honor

Unlike the Hall of Warriors, which celebrates Klingon soldiers and others with records of distinguished service to the Empire, the Hall of Honor offers respectful tribute to worthy adversaries vanquished in battle against Klingon warships. In keeping with the respect extended to these individuals, the Hall of Honor is but a short walk west from the Hall of Warriors, accessible by a cobblestone path running adjacent to the Qam-Chee River. Here, banners, flags, and other items salvaged from captured enemy vessels are on exhibit, each flanked by displays that recount the details of the glorious victory. As described by the Hall's curator, it is an honor to be memorialized here, though travelers with familial connections to anyone who may have served on—for example—a Starfleet ship that was captured or destroyed might feel differently. Visitors are encouraged to engage with the staff at every opportunity to learn the complete stories behind the artifacts housed here and discover more about the Klingon people's unique veneration of honorable opponents.

The Caves of No'Mat

Located deep within the mountainous region north of the city, these lava caves are famous for their restorative qualities. Many a Klingon has reported that the lava's heat coupled with intense meditation can induce powerful hallucinations that often aid an individual's attempts at "soul searching." The caves became so popular that a ceremonial ritual, the Rite of *MajQa*, evolved from the meditative practices. Visions experienced during this observance are believed to be of great import, especially if the Klingon undertaking the exercise believes he or she has communicated with a deceased family member or experienced a vision of his or her own future. The recent addition of a transparent duranium walkway allows visitors to hike deep into the caves just meters above the lava roiling upward from the caves' depths.

Museum of Reclaw

Given Kahless's enduring influence in Klingon history, it's easy to forget that other noteworthy emperors also ruled the Empire. Chief among these prominent monarchs is Reclaw, the last emperor of the Klingon Second Dynasty during what would have been the sixteenth century on Earth. At this museum located a short walk north of the Hall of

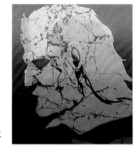

Warriors in the Old Quarter, you'll find a repository of documents, artifacts, and other items that trace Reclaw's reign. Unlike Kahless, who is renowned for uniting the Klingon people and roundly defeating most of those who would defy his rule, Reclaw's reign was fraught with attempts to overthrow him. According to records, which remain incomplete to this day, the First City was attacked at least four times by those challenging him for the throne. Holographic presentations re-create highlights from Reclaw's supremacy, which finally ended with his assassination at the hands of General K'Trelan during a coup d'état that ultimately led to the end of the Second Dynasty. In the wake of that takeover, K'Trelan appointed himself as Reclaw's successor, bringing an end to one of the more tumultuous periods in Klingon history. Guided tours of the museum have limited spaces and operate without reservations, so plan to arrive early.

🛍 SHOPPING AND ENTERTAINMENT

While appealing to non-Klingon residents and tourists has become a trend in recent decades, don't confuse the First City with some grand intergalactic melting pot. This is still the heart of the Klingon Empire, after all, which means you can expect the vast majority of restaurants and bars to have menus that cater directly to the locals. The regulars at various establishments will make no secret of their respect for an offworlder who demonstrates the courage to sample Klingon cuisine.

▲ Pao'La Open Air Bazaar

Located in the *Qav* Quarter in the city's southeastern region, this shopping area is one of the best places in the city to sample a broad cross section of clothing, decor, crafts, foods, and spirits from around the planet. Like the rest of the immediate area, the bazaar feels like a more recent addition to the First City, and its modern architecture and amenities make it the ideal location for retailers catering to tourists as well as locals. Restaurants and taverns abound, and street merchants offer a healthy selection of local and offworlder fare. One of the most popular venues is Rolatahk, which showcases what the eatery's proprietor, D'janoq, calls "*nItebHa' DuD*," or a blending of Klingon delicacies with classic human preparation and presentation. D'janoq has eschewed convention while winning awards and notices for his recipes, which call for cooking foods that are traditionally served raw or even live. Chief among his signature dishes is smoked *targ* and sautéed *gagh* bloodworms. Due to the increasing popularity of these fusion creations, Rolatahk now hosts regular cooking demonstrations and classes.

Soridiem's *Klin zha* Parlor

Round out your afternoon or evening in relaxed fashion by partaking in a friendly round of the popular Klingon game *Klin zha*. Favored by players of chess and other similar strategy games, *Klin zha* requires discipline and patience, along with forward thinking and a touch of guile. Soridiem's parlor is home to forty-seven tables that welcome players of all skill levels, and tournaments take place at least once a month. Offworlders are encouraged to participate, and despite the Klingons' competitive nature, physical fights are infrequent and actual fatalities are rarer still.

▲ *The Dream of the Fire*

Renowned Klingon author K'Ratak's celebrated novel of romance set against the backdrop of war during the Heroic Age receives a live adaptation from *Cho'tahk*, a talented family of Klingon performers who've entertained audiences for five generations. They offer two nightly performances in the Han'vral Amphitheater located at the north end of the Pao'La Bazaar. A narrator recites the book's framing sequences before stepping into shadow as the actors convey the rest of the story. The performances evoke everything about the novel that made it such a sensation for readers across the planet as well as on worlds throughout the quadrant. Thanks to the novel's popularity outside the Empire, *Cho'tahk* often welcomes guest performances from non-Klingon acting companies, such as the famed Second Quadrant Players and the Warp-Speed Classic Repertoire Company.

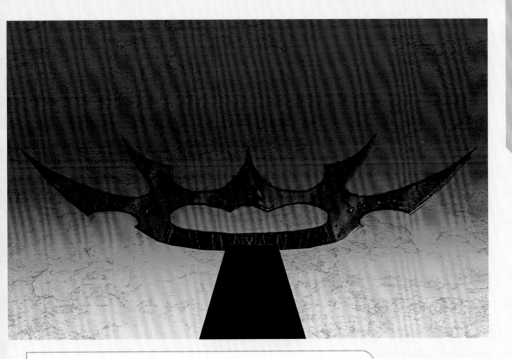

DID YOU KNOW?

THE SWORD OF KAHLESS

There are many enduring legends surrounding Kahless the Unforgettable that pit him against foes far more powerful than anything a mere mortal might hope to best. A number of these mythic tales involve Kahless creating mighty weapons with his bare hands—or through sheer force of will. The most celebrated of these creations, one that continues to embody all that it means to fight in service to the Klingon Empire, is the first *bat'leth*.

The storied blade has been the preferred weapon of Klingon warriors for centuries and is one of Kahless's enduring contributions to Klingon culture. In legends it is said that Kahless created the *bat'leth* himself after journeying to the Kri'stak Volcano and tossing a lock of his hair into the roiling lava at its core. He then took the lock, now burning with the intensity of a star gone nova, and cooled it in the soothing waters of the Lake of Lusor before forging the resulting metal into a distinctive blade of his own design.

Wielding this powerful new weapon, Kahless began eliminating his greatest enemies, including the malevolent tyrant Molor and the most formidable of the rival tribes, the Fek'lhri. Strengthened by those victories, Kahless then turned his attention to a far nobler purpose: building what would become the Klingon Empire. The sword itself has been lost to time, and while the legends surrounding the first emperor have expanded in number, scope, and whimsy over the centuries, the legacy of the Sword of Kahless is absolutely real and continues to serve as a symbol of unwavering Klingon strength and honor.

¶⊙¶ DINING AND NIGHTLIFE

Just in case this has somehow escaped your notice: Klingons like to drink. Most of them, anyway, and those who don't still like to have a good time. Because of that, finding a fun tavern or club to catch an evening drink is even easier than selecting a restaurant for dinner. There are hundreds of establishments scattered throughout the city, but the *Veb* and *wejDIch* Quarters are where you'll find the real action. Some of the bars can get fairly rowdy, though, in keeping with the finest Klingon traditions, and the locals pull no punches—figuratively *or* literally.

▼ 'Iwllj jachjaj

Classic and modern music vie for supremacy at this rowdy club in the *Veb* Quarter on the city's northwest side. Only here can you find opera played in one room while drinking songs dominate an adjacent chamber. Bloodwine, port, *warnog*, and *bi'jaTik* ale flow with abandon. It's also the only place in the city where you'll see nightly *gin'tak* throwing competitions. Everyone is invited to test their skill wielding these spears, which feature a knife blade at one end along with a blunt base that gives the weapon additional weight and power when used in close-quarter combat. Here, the goal is simple: Throw the *gin'tak* as far as you can. It's rare for a non-Klingon to win the contest, but don't let that stop you from giving it a go, as all enthusiastic competitors are welcomed.

Votaq's

Though everything on the menu is delicious, locals come here for this revered eatery's famous *rokeg*-blood pie. The primary ingredients of this delicacy are the flesh and thick, nutrient-rich blood of the *rokeg*, an amphibious predator indigenous to the River Skral that resembles the *gharials* of Trellus V (or an Earth crocodile) and can sometimes grow to a length exceeding five meters. It's said that Emperor Kaldon, while still a young warrior living along the river in the ninth century, slew such a *rokeg* using only his *d'k tahg* knife as a means of providing food for his village. His people had lost their homes and farms to torrential rains and the resulting floods and mudslides. The meal that resulted from Kaldon's courageous catch became a favorite repast for the remainder of his life and served as a reminder of his humble beginnings. In the generations since his reign, the dish has become a traditional meal during the Klingon Day of Honor. At Votaq's, bakers arrive hours before dawn each day to prepare five dozen such pies, which are only sold by the slice, one per customer with no exceptions; and once they're gone, you're out of luck until the next day. Anyone attempting to buck the house rules gets to face the diner's ill-tempered proprietor, Votaq himself, and if he decides you're too much trouble, that's when you meet his wife. Do yourself a favor, and enjoy your pie without the extra fuss.

▲ **Kiretek's Inn**

Gagh is one of a handful of Klingon foods that's well known beyond the Empire's borders. There are more than fifty different varieties of *gagh* bloodworms, and each is a unique delicacy. The type of animal blood the worms are fed as they are readied for consumption affects their taste, and not every variety of worm responds the same way to the blood it feasts on. It's a skilled chef who can provide a diverse selection of well-prepared *gagh* that appeals to multiple palates. Kiretek is just such a chef, and his is the only restaurant in the city that offers the entire range. All but hidden within the Old Quarter's garment district, this unassuming eatery is the destination of choice for many a *gagh* connoisseur. If you're feeling adventurous, just remember that *gagh* is best when served and consumed live, and many Klingons won't even consider eating cooked *gagh*. If you decide to follow the path of the purists, you'll probably want a mug of the inn's signature *warnog* to help eliminate any worms that survive the trip to your stomach. After all, it's best to nip them in the bud before they attach themselves to your intestines. Bon appétit!

🛏 LODGING

Accommodations are abundant within the city, ranging from quaint lodges and inns to state-of-the-art hotels with all the latest amenities. Though Klingons pride themselves on eschewing such luxury, that hasn't stopped savvy locals from developing properties that cater to the planet's growing tourism trade. No matter your physical requirements or desire for comfort, somewhere in the First City, there's a bed for you.

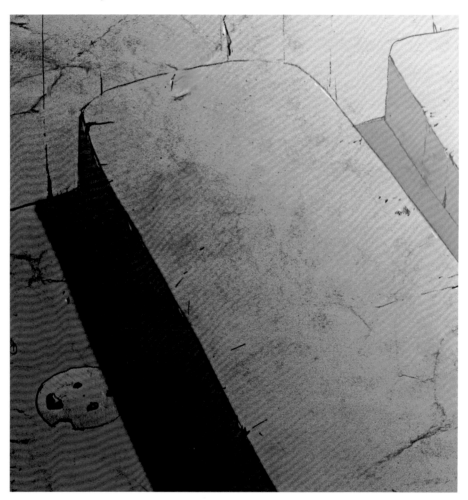

▲ Hapwlj nagh mebpa'mey

For those of you seeking an authentic Klingon experience, you've come to the right place. Translated to Standard, *Hapwlj nagh mebpa'mey* means "Flat Rock Hotel," an indication of what you're in for when you stay here. Instead of beds, guests sleep on stone slabs in keeping with Klingon tradition. The on-site restaurant features only local cuisine, including a wide variety of the live fare that so many Klingons relish. Be prepared for meals that cross the table to your plate.

Hotel Jarantine

A modern property on the inside, this hotel was converted from an ancient temple, which at one time was connected to the fortress that now serves as the Great Hall. Its proximity to the Hall makes it the preferred lodging for offworld diplomats, military leaders, and other prominent citizens during their stays on Qo'noS. The lowest level, located two stories below ground, was originally excavated as a secret underground shelter in the wake of the Hur'q invasion of Qo'noS and was used as a rally point for smuggling civilians out of the city. Today, it houses the expansive garden that provides vegetables and fruits for the hotel's three restaurants.

▲ Riverfront Enclave

Formerly a monastery for a small religious sect devoted to waiting for the promised return of Kahless from the afterlife, this collection of adobe brick cottages offers scenic views of the beautiful Qam-Chee River, which winds through the *wejDIch* and *Qav* Quarters on the city's south side. The sect was dissolved decades ago, but its archives remain. Guests are invited to tour the monastery grounds, which are maintained for their historical significance by clerics from surrounding temples. The library contains numerous texts penned by monks who once called the enclave home.

Several of the scrolls date back to the time of Kahless, offering one of the few surviving sources of accurate historical information from that period. Also housed here is one of the earliest known handwritten drafts of *The Story of the Promise*, which tells of Kahless's return. Enclave Fifteen carries its own bit of local lore, as it was here that famed author K'Ratak secreted himself in order to write *The Dream of the Fire*, which would go on to become one of the most prominent novels in Klingon literature.

THE CENTRAL PLAINS

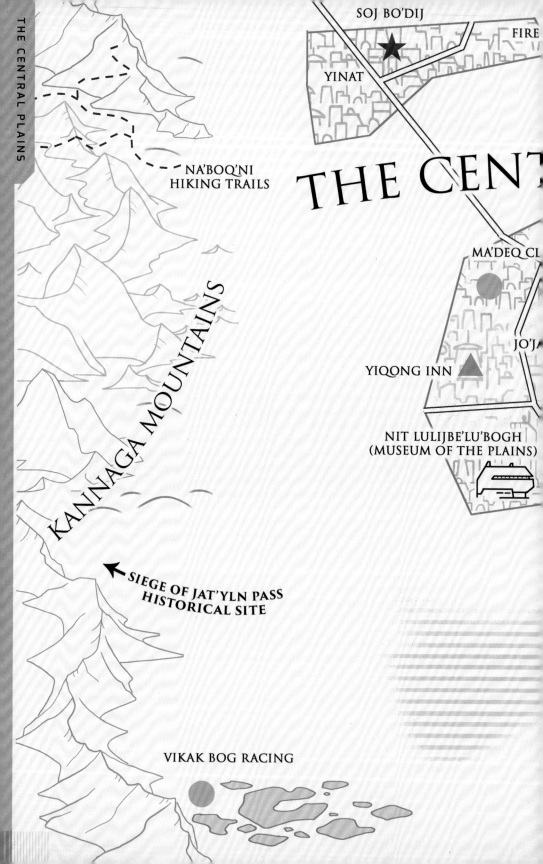

SOJ BO'DIJ

FIRE

YINAT

NA'BOQ'NI
HIKING TRAILS

THE CENT

MA'DEQ CL

YIQONG INN

JO'JA

KANNAGA MOUNTAINS

NIT LULIJBE'LU'BOGH
(MUSEUM OF THE PLAINS)

SIEGE OF JAT'YLN PASS
HISTORICAL SITE

VIKAK BOG RACING

N

NGS

RAL PLAINS

ERS

QEYLIS LOS
MONASTERY

TLHINGTUJ MOUNTAINS

THE TIPSY
TARG

BAS QAP
(METAL WORK)

RYS'TOH

HA'DIBAH
(MEAT)

BRO'TANG RIVER

SHOPPING &
RECREATION

DINING &
NIGHTLIFE

LODGING

NOT HOME TO ANY MAJOR METROPOLITAN AREAS, the Central Plains region is a stretch of country occupying the middle portion of the planet's supercontinent, acting as a natural buffer between the Kannaga and Tlhlngtuj mountain ranges that run north to south along the continent's western and eastern reaches.

In the time before airborne transportation, the Plains served as a trade corridor linking the First City with destinations such as Quin'lat and other villages and provinces to the north, with numerous small villages and settlements springing up along the major trade routes. The trains and other overland conveyances that linked these outposts became prime targets for marauders and bandits, as well as rogue tribes who continued to resist efforts to unite under the banner of the emerging Klingon Empire. Life in these "frontier towns" was, and remains, simple, with an emphasis on agriculture, hunting, and fishing, and even the arts. Despite the popular notion that Klingons die with their boots on, it's not uncommon to encounter retired warriors in the Central Plains, seeking respite from a lifetime of service and battle and opting to live out their remaining years in peace.

 GETTING AROUND

There are hundreds of small villages scattered throughout the area, though most of them are little more than a handful of families living in clusters of simple homes. In order to shop and trade, residents generally travel to the larger communities of Jo'jahQ, Yinat, or Rys'toH. Moving between the different villages along the major trade route will require some form of overland or air transportation, but once you arrive at your destination, you will generally find that mag-rail stations, heliports, and other mass transit hubs are within walking distance. A good pair of hiking boots will serve you well during these excursions. Dining options may be limited depending on which area you are visiting, and accommodations will almost always involve traditional Klingon sleeping arrangements.

THE CENTRAL PLAINS: A WORLD APART

[First published in the 2291 Edition]
One thing I have always tried to do, first as a member of the High Council and later after I ascended to the position of chancellor, is showcase the many sides of Klingon society. For too long, the Empire has been viewed as nothing more than a fascist military state, interested in nothing but war and conquest. That has certainly been true for the majority of the Empire's existence, and our reputation as a force of great power is well earned. However, there are many other facets of our civilization that rarely receive notice, even now that we have moved beyond the outdated ways of simply seizing from others for the glory of the Empire.

For example, there are the people of the Central Plains. Here, distant from the political spectacle that can consume our leadership in the First City, and far away even from the industrial frenzy that so characterizes Krennla, Quin'lat, and other cities vital to our global and interstellar economy, is a segment of Klingon life seldom seen by outsiders. You'll find a host of farmers and artists and other skilled craftspeople in this region, proud of the work they do and the lives they lead. There are no military bases or garrisons here, nor fleets of warships staged for battle. Instead, in the Central Plains, one is better able to appreciate the gifts our world gives us while respectfully taking from the land only that which is needed to live. However, we Klingons in the region are still able to seek adventure and pit ourselves against the challenges nature itself provides. Why venture to the stars in search of enemies, real or perceived, when our planet stands ready to put our hunting and fighting prowess to the ultimate test?

There are those who might argue that the region and its rural culture are, by their very nature, out of place on Qo'noS, but the Klingons who call the Central Plains home treasure their heritage with the same passion as any warrior. Their ancestors fought to make a life for themselves and their families, holding themselves to the same standards of honor and courage espoused by our people throughout history. As our relationship with the Federation and other interstellar powers continues to evolve, it is my fervent hope that more outsiders can come to appreciate the breadth of qualities Klingon society has to offer, and the Central Plains exemplifies this cultural diversity.

—Gorkon, Chancellor of the Klingon High Council

👁 SIGHTS AND ACTIVITIES

While "no frills" might not accurately describe the Central Plains region, it's worth noting that you're not going to find much in the way of tourist-friendly points of interest in this part of the world. However, those with an appreciation for history will find plenty to draw their attention given this area's role in the advancement of Klingon society. There also are a number of historical sites that bore witness to the planet's violent past, including the chaos surrounding the Empire's pre-history. You'll find that while the locals are dedicated to the preservation of such sites and artifacts, they're not terribly interested in showcasing that aspect of their homeland. Instead, be ready for a tour of the latest crop from their *pe'bot* orchard!

▲ nIt lulljbe'lu'bogh

In Federation Standard, "Memories of the Plains." The only museum of its type in the entire region is located in the village of Jo'jahQ, which lies near the halfway point on the main overland route between the First City and Quin'lat. Here you'll find a small yet well-tended exhibit highlighting the history of the area and the struggles of the region's original settlers, many of whom came from tribes opposed to Kahless and his attempts to form an Empire. Still others were from communities caught between tribes more interested in defeating each other than with the innocent victims who became collateral damage. Once Kahless succeeded in his efforts to unify many of the tribes who called this region home, war began shifting away from the territory. This eventually opened up opportunities to expand trade from the capital toward other isolated provinces. The museum's most overt nod to the region's sometimes brutal past lies in a subterranean chamber where the skulls and weapons of enemy fighters from rival tribes still hang on the stone walls.

▲ Fire Springs

Among the area's more closely guarded secrets are the hot springs located near the small village of Yinat. Fewer than one hundred people live in the community, which receives the bulk of its goods and trade from Jo'jahQ, one hundred or so kilometers to the south. At the fire springs, channels carved through volcanic rock carry water upward from the underground rivers into more than a dozen natural pools. Visitors are welcome to partake of the springs, which are said to have an excellent restorative effect on the body. The remains of a small, primitive community tucked into the neighboring foothills are from an earlier attempt to settle the area, perhaps in a bid to control the water source. During cooler months, the springs are a popular gathering place for the locals as well as friends from the surrounding villages. It's a favored location for the *Bre'Nan*, a ritual that's performed prior to a wedding ceremony, during which the matriarch of the groom's family provides formal approval for her son's bride to join his House.

▼ qeylIS loS

This monastery, located several kilometers east of Jo'jahQ and established 1,500 years ago, is staffed by clerics who live on the grounds in a cluster of small hand-carved brick buildings and regard themselves as the "guardians of prophecy." Abiding by the teachings of Kahless and the promise he made to one day return from *Sto-Vo-Kor* to lead the Klingon people, the monks established the monastery directly beneath the star that the first emperor prophesized would be the location of his reappearance. Following the arrival of Kahless's clone in 2369, just eighteen years ago, the clerics on Qo'noS continue to await the return of the "real" Kahless. The monastery's mission has evolved throughout the years to include historical preservation of their work, and visitors will find handwritten texts dating back centuries that chronicle the monastery's teachings as well as the challenges they sometimes face trying to spread their message to nonbelievers.

DID YOU KNOW?

THE STORY OF THE PROMISE

One of the greatest legends in all of Klingon lore, *The Story of the Promise* is the tale of Kahless the Unforgettable's vow that he would come back to the world of the living in order to rule the Empire once again. As the story goes, he pointed to a distant star and proclaimed, "Seek me there, for there I shall return."

Long before the notion of spaceflight and journeying to other worlds became a reality, some Klingons construed Kahless's declaration to mean they should venture into the wilderness of Qo'noS, seeking the spot beneath that star and guarding it until the day of the emperor's return. There are many who believe it was this quest that fueled the original migration into the Central Plains and continued to attract many faithful acolytes for generations. However, many years later, sacred texts were unearthed that asserted Kahless had chosen the precise location of his return: the lava caves on the planet Boreth. There has since been much debate on this topic as to the veracity of such claims and their sources, and the arguments over the first emperor's intentions are unlikely to be settled any time soon. Regardless, *The Story of the Promise* remains perhaps the most recounted and revered legend in all of Klingon history.

▼ Na'boq'nI Hiking Trails

According to lore, this network of trails and paths winding through the foothills was used by the Na'boq'nI, a tribe of savage Klingon nomads who brutally opposed early attempts at expanding trade through the Central Plains region. Using the trails, some of them little more than narrow depressions caused by years of foot travel, Na'boq'nI warriors were able to move with startling speed to flank and ambush cargo convoys traversing the area. In modern times, a number of these paths now crisscross the region close to the larger settlements. Jo'jahQ in particular has a number of these smaller paths that give hikers access to secluded streams and ponds that are ideal for swimming and afternoon picnics; they also lead to caves in the foothills that are ripe for exploring. However, the locals recommend traveling in groups and only during daylight hours, as it's not uncommon to stumble across a stray *ngem veqlargh*, or "brush devil," after sunset. These small predators prefer to hunt under cover of night, their dark, leatherlike hides allowing them to blend with the forest undergrowth. Despite their size, brush devils are aggressive and will use their long, bladelike teeth to attack when threatened, so be sure to give them a wide berth.

baS Qap

"Metal work." Venture to this dilapidated metal shack just beyond the western boundary of Rys'toH, a small fishing community forty kilometers south of Jo'jahQ. There you can watch Klingon blacksmiths forge tools, weapons, and other implements from wrought iron, steel, and other metals. Day in and day out, they toil in the face of the withering heat generated by a unique aqueduct system that channels geothermal energy from deep beneath the nearby TlhIngtuj Mountains. All items are created using traditional handcrafting methods that have been employed by the people of the Plains for uncounted generations. Though the shop's main priority is serving the needs of the community, in recent years the workers have started catering to tourists, and now baS Qap employs two blacksmiths just for the purpose of turning out various Klingon symbols and emblems for sale. However, please be warned that requests for *bat'leth* replicas will be turned down—often rudely. The fashioning of most Klingon weapons isn't something typically shared with offworlders, and that's especially true of the *bat'leth*. The process is enshrouded in as much mystery and legend as the blade's origins, and the art and craft of its forging is almost never demonstrated for non-Klingons. However, other popular items are available for purchase, including metal flutes used to attract the attention of *'etlh SIQ*, or "saber bears," during hunts in the surrounding mountains and foothills. If you end up buying one, we suggest not actually using it until you're well away from this region.

Siege of Jat'yln Pass Historical Site

The scars from one of the pivotal battles of the Empire's Second Dynasty still run deep in this stretch of jungle tucked within the foothills of the Kannaga Mountains. It was here, during the last years of the Second Dynasty, that famed military commander Kam'pok led a party of Klingon foot soldiers on a surprise assault against the forces of Kovatch, the general of a rival army and leader of the House of Zin'zeQ, who attempted a coup d'état to usurp Emperor Reclaw. Kam'pok's strategy of deploying a small, rapidly moving force against a larger enemy contingent was unheard of in that day and age, and many of his superiors scoffed at the notion. Paying the doubters no heed, Kam'pok put his plan into motion, striking hard and fast while employing bold, unconventional tactics that gained immediate success against Kovatch's numerically superior forces. Despite his own death in face-to-face combat with Kovatch, Kam'pok's strategy was successful. The uprising was quelled and Reclaw held on to his throne, at least for a time. The battle continues to be cited as a timeless example of audacious military tactics and is still taught as part of the small-unit combat curriculum at the veS DuSaQ military academy. A small glade that marks Jat'yln Pass, where the bulk of the fierce ground battle took place, is maintained as a historical site, forever marked for preservation so that future generations can learn and appreciate the fearlessness of one Klingon commander who dared to defy convention.

DID YOU KNOW?

qeS'a': THE KLINGON ART OF WAR

That Klingons spend an inordinate amount of time fighting and training to fight goes without saying. Often overlooked is just how much time and energy Klingon soldiers devote to the *study* of warfare.

Every warrior, regardless of rank or position, is required each year to revisit the principles and lessons contained in the seminal volume *qeS'a': The Klingon Art of War*. Believed by some to be written by Kahless himself, the truth is that the author of this timeless text remains unknown. Despite this lingering mystery, *qeS'a'* is widely regarded as one of the cornerstone texts on the proper conduct of war.

Written as a military text, other parties—Klingon and offworlder alike—have found ways to adapt the sacred teachings into other walks of life, such as business and politics. In the centuries since its discovery and initial publication, *qeS'a'* has remained readily available, and its lessons continue to be scrutinized, debated, argued, and fought over by historians, scholars, and warriors.

🧳 SHOPPING AND ENTERTAINMENT

Farmers, tailors, craftspeople, and artists tend to drive the economy in most of the smaller settlements along the Central Plains' major trade corridors. Although the region also receives a steady stream of imported goods, you won't enjoy the same broad selection you'd find in the major cities. Don't worry if you don't have money to splurge; bartering works just as well in most cases, and even volunteering to help a merchant move crates or pallets of goods from storehouse to market square can earn you a bushel of fruit or some fresh *plpuS pach* (also known as *pipius* claw) for lunch. Entertainment options might seem limited at first, but as you explore the area you'll realize that each of the villages has its own charm. The people of Yinat take their evening festivities to the narrow streets outside their homes and well into the night, while the villagers of Rys'toH prefer mid-morning merriment after local fishermen catch their daily quota of *jytrios*, the large eel-like creatures that call the nearby Bro'tahg River home. Visitors are reminded to respect such community customs when visiting these areas.

Vikak Bog Racing

The jungle swamps that envelop the foothills south of the Kannaga Mountains have, for centuries, proven to be challenging terrain for hunters and trackers. Generations ago, outlaw bands would evade law enforcement by hiding deep within the thick undergrowth, and it's said that Commander Kam'pok also used the unforgiving landscape to his advantage during his legendary defeat of General Kovath's forces at the Siege of Jat'yln Pass. Today the region still serves as a prime hunting ground, but also a place for a unique brand of overland racing. Locals employ Vikak—oversized, six-wheeled all-terrain vehicles—to navigate a five-hundred-kilometer course through the dense jungle and pitiless marshlands over a three-day period. Along the way, the two-person driving teams face not only the dangers the land provides in the way of terrain and predatory animals, but also traps, obstacles, and even ambushes sprung by designated "enemy marauders"—Klingon troublemakers employed to add an extra element of danger to the race. Visitors are invited to observe the race, either as part of a special tour group or—if they're feeling bold—as the partner of an experienced Klingon driver.

▲ Ma'deQ Clothiers

The largest supplier of imported and locally made garments and accessories in the region is found here in this simple, unassuming shop in Jo'jahQ's northern quarter. The shop's proprietor, B'ervath, presents the work of around three dozen local tailors and seamstresses who provide their creations on consignment, allowing shoppers to peruse a variety of styles in addition to more conventional clothing brought in from the larger cities. Whether you're shopping for a warm robe to protect against the elements, leather hunting leggings that'll protect you from the teeth of a saber bear, or a sheath for your d'k tahg knife, Ma'deQ has you covered. B'ervath is known to haggle once in a while, too, so don't be surprised if she makes you an offer on the shirt you're wearing.

¡©¡ DINING AND NIGHTLIFE

If you're looking for fine dining, you're in the wrong place and should probably take one of the mag-rails back to the city. That's not to say you won't find good cooking out here. The locals take pride in their various twists on Klingon cuisine, and a few have even become interested in creating offworld dishes in a bid to attract visitors. Be prepared for a lot of big meals that involve plenty of meat (some of it cooked, if you're lucky) and heavy starches. You'll find that most of the eateries in the various towns and villages of the Central Plains source their ingredients locally, so as often as not there will be just one entree on the menu, consisting of meat from whatever game animals were successfully hunted that day.

▼ Soj bo'DIj

An eclectic selection of cuisine characterizes this open-air buffet that has become one of Yinat's most enduring traditions. There's no better way to finish off a day at the Fire Springs than with a healthy repast from one of the eight different vendors who set up shop here. It's a sure bet that you'll be lured by the smell of fresh-baked *JInjoq* bread, and it's not uncommon to find a freshly slain *targ* on a spit over a low fire, the heat just enough to bring out the beast's natural flavor without actually fully cooking the meat. Wash all of it down with a mug of homebrewed *warnog*, which is available by the barrel.

▼ Ha'DIbaH

Simply put? "Meat." You won't find a single vegetable or piece of fruit anywhere, not even as decoration, in this small, ramshackle cafe near the Rys'toH village square. Rumor has it the occasional piece of bread infiltrates the premises, but there has yet to be a confirmed sighting. The meat-lover's menu runs heavy with the likes of *pipius* claw and *jytrios* eel, *Ilngta'* breast, *krada* legs doused in the hottest *grapok* sauce we've ever tasted, and—of course—*gagh* in its many flavorful forms. Heart of *targ* is a specialty item, only served during holidays and festivals. Wash everything down with the cafe's signature ale that's crafted on the premises, or dunk your head in one of the many, *many* available casks of bloodwine.

The Tipsy Targ

A classic Klingon tavern of the old school variety, located across the street from the offices of Jo'jahQ's provincial government at the center of town. If you're looking for a fancy cocktail, you are most definitely in the wrong place. However, you can avoid the chorus of mocking laughter from the bartender if you stick to ordering drinks that only consist of one element: bloodwine. The "Double T" does have a food menu that includes an assortment of vegetables and fruits if you're not into live *gagh* or *bregit* lung. If you ask nicely, the cook might even agree to place a cut of *TKnag* steak over an open flame for a minute or two.

DID YOU KNOW?
THE MUAR'TEK FESTIVAL

Klingons don't really need a reason to throw a party, but having justification just makes everything that much more fun. The annual Muar'tek Festival is one such observance, with parties, parades, carnivals, and other activities taking place around the planet. Three days of celebration honor the establishment of modern Klingon civilization, which is generally recognized as an age of enlightenment that began during the mid-twenty-first century. The festival is observed all over the planet and, in the Central Plains, hundreds gather to celebrate at the Fire Springs near the village of Yinat. The pyrotechnic displays set off above the Tlhlngtuj Mountains can be seen throughout the region, and the music is carried on the night air to many of the surrounding villages. Though the celebration used to prohibit non-Klingons, the increased interest from offworld tourists has led community leaders to relax local standards and welcome anyone who wishes to celebrate all it means to be Klingon.

🛏 LODGING

Several of the taverns have accommodations, and the larger villages along the main travel corridor do have a small selection of lodges and inns, but you can forget finding anything that might be considered luxurious or even comfortable. It's all traditional Klingon sleeping arrangements out here, but some proprietors have been known to take pity on weary offworlders and provide hay or straw-filled burlap mattresses to go with the stone or metal sleeping slabs. That said, be sure to inspect any bedding you might receive, as Tashmanian spiders and other pesky insects are a common complaint. On the other hand, if you can capture one of the spiders, they taste great when deep-fried.

▲ ylQong Inn

As you've probably guessed by now, Klingons aren't big on fancy names to describe simple services, and the "Sleep Inn" is no exception. The closest thing to any sort of restful lodging along the main trade route is located in Jo'jahQ, tucked inside a warehouse that was completely gutted thirty years ago and renovated to serve as a hotel. It's the town's answer to "tourist-friendly accommodations," which means it's a step or two up from sleeping on the ground in the rain. The rooms are small—so small that many Klingons actually forgo them in favor of sleeping outside—and contain sleeping slabs, which can be augmented with thin mattresses available for rent from Datoq, the elderly Klingon innkeeper. Meals are included in the modest nightly rate, and Datoq is attentive enough to guest needs, if a little surly. We recommend avoiding him until he's had his first cup of morning *raktajino*, lest you rile him and get a *bat'leth* through your hotel room door.

SIDE TRIP: KHITOMER

Even the most casual followers of Klingon history know about the outpost on the planet Khitomer and the rather unlikely role it played in easing the tumultuous period of political tension between the Empire and the Federation during the late twenty-third century. Used as a forward military installation because of its proximity to the Empire's border with Federation space, for years Khitomer served as an early warning outpost in the event of Starfleet incursion into Klingon territory.

However, following the destruction of the Praxis moon in 2293 and the resulting environmental damage inflicted upon Qo'noS, the planet would play host to the first serious discussions of peace between the two powers. It galled many members of the High Council to even consider asking the Federation for assistance, but the steady, thoughtful leadership of Chancellor Gorkon won over the dissenters.

Despite the massive shift in attitude such change would require, many came to believe that Gorkon would lead the Klingon people out of the crisis and into a bold new future, as allies of the Federation. Gorkon paid for his convictions with his life at the hands of dishonorable conspirators working from both within and outside the Empire, but his daughter, Azetbur, took up her father's cause. Just two months after the Praxis explosion, Azetbur presided over the signing of the Khitomer Treaty, which ensured peace between the Klingon Empire and the Federation. While the agreement would be tested in the years to come, most historians consider that day to be the point at which the two great powers took their first steps toward lasting peace.

Khitomer would bear witness to a strengthening of the Empire's new bond with its Federation allies a mere four decades later, when Romulans launched a surprise attack on the outpost. The unprovoked action resulted in the deaths of hundreds of Klingons, with scores more captured by Romulan soldiers. Once again, it was the Federation that provided assistance, without question or hesitation. The aid came in many forms, from providing emergency medical care, food, water, and shelter, to the adoption by Federation personnel of a handful of orphaned Klingon children. One of these youths, Worf, would grow up with a unique understanding of life as both a Klingon and a member of the Federation when, in 2361, he became the first Klingon to be commissioned as a Starfleet officer.

The legacy of Khitomer is one of tragedy and triumph, and it occupies a special place in the history of the Klingon people.

GETTING AROUND

In addition to its historical significance and ongoing use as a joint military outpost and location for diplomatic summits and other important, high-security events, Khitomer also functions as a retreat for ranking government officials, including the Federation President. Because of this, access to the outpost and its support facilities is carefully controlled. The rest of this small yet lush, green world is all but uninhabited and off-limits to visitors, though there are large training areas reserved for use by both Starfleet and Klingon Defense Force personnel. Sentry satellites along with a sensor network and a squadron of military patrol vessels ensure that no unauthorized traffic approaches the planet. Tours of the outpost are only conducted for groups in which all members have passed background checks. Chartered transport vessels arrive and dock at a single location, and arrival and departure schedules offer little room for deviation. Once you're on the ground, stay with your group at all times and observe all instructions from your guides or members of the facility staff. Tours of the Klingon military and Starfleet installations are not available.

SIGHTS AND ACTIVITIES

The main attraction here is the Grand Hall, which is the centerpiece of the Klingon and Starfleet presence on Khitomer. Despite its origins as a humble military outpost, the hall, along with the entire building and surrounding grounds, has continued to benefit from renovation and expansion over the years. Both the Empire and the Federation have devoted resources toward its preservation as both a historical site and a gathering place for matters of great import.

▲ Atrium of Reflection

The foyer leading to the Grand Hall is almost as beautiful as the building's central chamber. Artwork and sculpture from numerous Klingon and Federation worlds decorate the immense chamber, and its outer walls of transparent tritanium offer unfettered views of the lake to the east, along with the sunsets that illuminate the mountain range and valleys beyond. Used for a variety of ceremonial purposes, the atrium is witness to a wide range of important events, from award presentations and military promotions to the lying-in-state of distinguished citizens. The atrium also includes a Gallery of Remembrance featuring statues of past Klingon chancellors and Federation presidents.

The Chamber of Voices

Though the availability of subspace communication renders large assemblies of the quadrant's planetary leaders somewhat wasteful, there is a feeling of tremendous significance whenever occasion calls for them to congregate here in person. You can almost feel the power of history itself embracing you as you step from the Atrium of Reflection into this massive assembly hall. Banners and flags from all the worlds of the Empire decorate high stone walls that angle upward before culminating in a transparent dome that illuminates the chamber floor. Visitors are allowed access to the chamber when no official activities are scheduled, and holographic projectors offer recorded presentations of more than a dozen landmark speeches and debates from the past century. Some of those available for viewing include the signing of the Khitomer Accords in 2295, Chancellor K'mpec's 2346 call to renew the Empire's commitment to peace with the Federation, and President Min Zife's impassioned plea in 2373 for the Empire to mend its alliance with the Federation so that both powers could stand together against the Dominion. These presentations can be observed from the main floor or the observer's gallery overlooking the Chamber.

Khitomer Peace Park

The grounds surrounding the Grand Hall have recently undergone a complete renovation, with expanded gardens able to accommodate flora not just from Klingon and Federation worlds but also vegetation from the planets of newer allies. Specimens of Cardassian and even Romulan flowers and plants now decorate the lovingly tended estate, blending with the existing vegetation to marvelous effect. The recent additions serve to highlight the persistent, evolving nature of the peace process and how it ultimately triumphs and forges lasting bonds between once-bitter enemies. Visitors are invited to spend time in quiet reflection, or take advantage of guided tours of the grounds, which are available throughout the day. The peace park is bordered on its east side by an immense artificial lake, which also provides hydroelectric power to the Grand Hall and neighboring buildings.

DID YOU KNOW?
KOR, KOLOTH, AND KANG: WITNESSES TO HISTORY

There are few who occupy such revered places in the annals of Klingon history as these three renowned warriors. Each joined the Klingon Defense Force at a young age, when the Empire was still at odds with its then-greatest rival, the Federation. All three share the distinction of having been bested by one of the Federation's most notable military leaders, Captain James T. Kirk, though each would claim they carry no dishonor having been defeated at the hands of a worthy adversary. Before eventually falling in battle, all three lived long enough to amass considerable accolades for distinguished service and to witness the signing of the Khitomer Accords. In the finest fashion of loyal soldiers forever sworn to obey the citizenry they protect, they each died fighting alongside Starfleet, upholding the bonds of peace forged from the melted chains of distrust and aggression.

In war and peace, standing against old enemies or with new allies, Kor, Koloth, and Kang remain shining examples of both the Empire's past and the promise of its future.

🛍️ SHOPPING AND ENTERTAINMENT

Retail establishments are notably lacking here, but the book and sundries shop located on the Grand Hall's ground level will likely cover your basic needs. Replicas of treaties and other significant documents drafted or signed in the Grand Hall can also be purchased, along with original art and ornamental sculptures inspired by the architecture and monuments found at the outpost. There's also a large selection of books, which includes biographies and historical texts written by notable figures with ties to Khitomer.

🍽️ DINING

The Grand Hall features an award-winning dining facility that's home to ten different vendors offering traditional Klingon cuisine, as well as selections from more than a dozen Federation worlds. For non-Klingons longing for a taste of home, this menu will be a real treat.

▲ **Raktajino Cafe**

Though Klingon coffee is the name of the game here, you'll also find Earth and other prominent worlds well represented in this small cafe located just off the Atrium of Reflection. The diverse and attentive staff is ready to provide for even the most particular of coffee tastes. Every cup here is prepared to each customer's exacting standards and brewed with fresh beans imported each week. True coffee aficionados will love the signature "Khitomer Express," a tasty, locally sourced blend exclusive to the Raktajino Cafe, with ingredients so secret that the recipe isn't even available for replicators. For those who prefer tea, the cafe also offers a variety of—among many others—human, Vulcan, and Klingon blends, along with one of the best *targ* panini you'll find anywhere in the Empire.

KRENNLA

N

QO'D

KR

LE'DAQH
THEATER

GEJAL'TOH
HOTEL

JAWBE' CHEN
(AMONG THE CLOUDS)

CU
OU
C

BALDI'MAJ DISTRICT

T'JOBHAV P

KRAVOK
MONUM

SUT HABMOHWI' SARGH
(THE IRON HORSE)

HOUSE OF VARNAK

MOUNTAINS

NNLA

KRENNLA SPACEPORT

AL
CH

KAS'CA'S MARKET

VOKAR'S
TARG HOUSE

VES DUSAO
(SCHOOL OF WAR)

QAQ NITLH ROS

TA DISTRICT

SHOPPING &
RECREATION

DINING &
NIGHTLIFE

LODGING

AS INDUSTRIALIZATION TOOK HOLD ON QO'NOS, several prominent family Houses struck out from the First City, traversing the supercontinent to the planet's farthest regions in a bid to make their own mark on the still-young Klingon Empire. Immense power production facilities were constructed around Qo'noS, taking advantage of abundant geothermal energy and the planet's ceaseless volcanic activity. The power generated from these installations was channeled to the larger population centers and other settlements, allowing significant growth as technology advanced. Entire cities sprang up around these facilities to support their operation, in turn generating a wide range of businesses that would cater to the workers, other residents, and—eventually—visitors from other worlds.

As time passed and the tenets of the Klingon Empire took hold, rapid advances in technology and shifts in economic interests caused several cities to stagnate and eventually die out. Meanwhile, Krennla was one of the few regions that continued to adapt over time to changing demands and goals. Though several of the Houses that had originally settled the area had at first allowed themselves to become mired in a seemingly unending series of feuds and other petty disputes, two families, the House of Nrie and the House of Y'dnirak, eventually united and channeled their joint power into stabilizing the region. Their influence soon spread beyond Qo'noS, opening up trade with planets across the quadrant and prompting the construction of a massive spaceport along the city's eastern boundary. This, along with the rise of the tourist trade on Qo'noS, has helped to transform Krennla into a transportation hub for passengers and cargo being shipped to and from the home world.

Located in the northern half of the supercontinent in the flatlands south of the Qo'dung Mountains, Krennla enjoys a climate that's moderate and cooler than that of the First City and its surrounding areas and other regions south of the Kannaga Mountain Range. Unlike the capital and other larger metropolitan areas that feature many nods to history and tradition, Krennla is a very utilitarian municipality. The bulk of the city was built with an eye toward the industry it supports and was divided into boroughs or districts that, over time, have served to segregate the city's population based on socioeconomic status. Almost out of place is the Baldi'maj District on the west side, which carries with it a stately "old money" vibe as home to the renowned family Houses that helped found the city. Their wealthy descendants still populate a broad section of the area today.

Elsewhere in the city, you may be able to find upscale dining or lodging options, but don't expect the broad selection you might enjoy in other metropolitan areas. War monuments and other historical sites on the city's outskirts are the main attraction for visitors, and locals are very welcoming to outsiders.

 GETTING AROUND

Mass transit via transporter is the order of the day in Krennla. The majority of the population lives in high-rise apartment towers arrayed in clusters throughout the city. On a precise schedule throughout the day, automated transporter hub stations transfer commuters in large groups from these clusters to designated transfer points. Traffic from the spaceport prohibits the use of personal airborne vehicles, and traveling to historical sites on the city's fringes requires the use of rail lines or other ground conveyance. Those who prefer a refreshing walk in the open air can avail themselves of the kilometers of walking paths that weave through the city, offering unfettered views of vast stretches of botanical gardens and other green spaces that serve as buffers against the encroaching buildings and infrastructure.

KRENNLA:
MY UNEXPECTED HOME

[First published in the 2381 Edition]
I was born and raised on Kessik IV and never even visited Qo'noS until after my eighth birthday. Being the offspring of a human male and Klingon female made me an aberration to many older Klingons, despite the fact that the thawing of relations between the Empire and the Federation was already well under way by the time I was born. I was raised among humans on a Federation colony, so of course I developed many human mannerisms, attitudes, and habits. Because of this, any time we visited my mother's family on the Homeworld, things tended to be awkward for me.

Thankfully, there was my grandfather.

A worker in the primary factory in Krennla, he was a loyal, diligent Klingon who never missed a day's work. He also saw to it that I never felt like an outsider. Thanks to him, I came to appreciate the city and its history, and the role it played in the Empire's technological advancements. I also learned how the Klingon people opened our borders and arms to those who were once our enemy. As someone who often feels like a bridge between two races, I was grateful to my grandfather for showing me the best aspects of Klingon society.

When visiting Krennla, many tourists are naturally drawn to the Baldi'maj District, which is more upscale thanks to the older, richer families living there; however, I never cared for that part of the city. For me, the downtown district is where Krennla comes alive. This is a part of the city that never really goes to sleep, and the hustle of activity is constant—you can shop, or eat, or find a drink at any hour of the day or night. T'jobhaV Park, located in the city center, is beautiful at night, with a waterfall and streams that wind through the wooded areas almost making you forget that you're surrounded by high-rise towers. To this day, it's still my favorite place to visit.

It may not be as ostentatious or wrapped within the veils of history as the First City or other prominent destinations on Qo'noS, but don't let its workmanlike demeanor fool you. Krennla has a charm you won't find anywhere else.

—Lieutenant Commander B'Elanna Torres, *U.S.S. Voyager*

SIGHTS AND ACTIVITIES

Though some might dismiss Krennla as a largely working-class city with little regard for cultural pursuits, the city is home to numerous historical locations and other significant points of interest that are well worth exploring. Take at least part of a day to wander around the Baldi'maj District, located on the city's western outskirts, where upscale shopping, dining, and entertainment options cater to the city's more affluent residents.

▼ House of Varnak

One of the oldest and most influential families on the planet, the House of Varnak, made its home in Krennla, located in what later became the Kenta District on the city's south side. The House's reign continued for nearly seven hundred years but came to an abrupt end in 2375, after its patriarch, Koradan, made the unwise decision to support the overthrow of Chancellor Martok. The coup Koradan supported was launched by Martok's son, Morjod, and when it failed, Martok saw to it that the House of Varnak was abolished and every member of the family executed. The magnificent citadel that was once the family home has since been converted into a museum dedicated to memorializing the coup attempt and the heavy price paid by those who participated in the uprising. It also serves a second purpose, standing as a warning to anyone who might consider similar foolhardy action against a chancellor or the High Council.

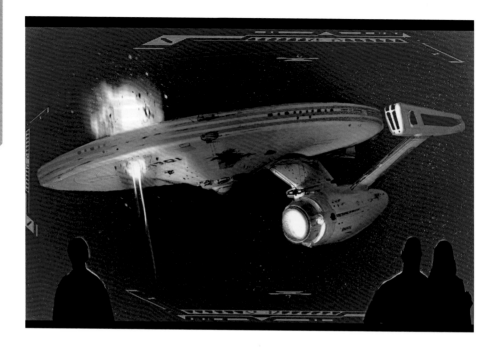

▲ Cultural Outreach Center

In perhaps one of the most overt attempts by locals to showcase the culture of the Klingon people to the ever-growing numbers of tourists who visit Krennla each year, this visitors center and its various programs and initiatives have been a resounding success with offworlders. Located near the northern edge of T'jobhaV Park in the heart of the city, the center features guided tours through more than a dozen exhibits that showcase various turning points in Klingon history. The milestones represented here include the reign of Kahless and the growth of the Empire beyond Qo'noS; first contact and the Empire's continued strife with the Federation; the planet's struggles in the face of alien occupation; global environmental calamity in the aftermath of the Praxis moon explosion; and the Dominion war and the modern era of Chancellor Martok. The information is presented without flourish, shunning embellishment or propaganda in favor of a straightforward recounting that even covers parts of Klingon history that offworlders might find unsettling. This is particularly true with respect to the sections devoted to the expansion of the Empire through war and conquest. Daily demonstrations of various ceremonies include the Rite of Ascension (see page opposite). If you happen to be visiting during the midday meal break, you may be able to witness or even participate in the Plea for the Dead, a prayer ritual conducted in memory of those who have left this world for *Sto-Vo-Kor*. The ceremony pays respect to deceased family members and close comrades, recognizing the sacrifices made by these loved ones and assuring their place in the afterlife.

DID YOU KNOW?
THE RITE OF ASCENSION

Even in a society that places such importance on military might, not every Klingon opts to become a soldier of the Empire. In order to begin that process, one must formally declare this intention in one of the most important and revered rituals in all of Klingon culture, the Rite of Ascension. This custom marks the first steps of a Klingon child who has chosen to follow the warrior's path.

The rite is composed of two ceremonies, the first held when a child reaches adolescence (approximately thirteen Earth years), at which time they declare their intention to become a warrior. This is accomplished by lighting a *kor'tova*, the candle's flame signifying the fire of the warrior's heart. Ten years after this initial ceremony, the child must then complete the final part of the ritual, the Second Rite of Ascension, in which he or she faces a gauntlet of warriors, each wielding *painstiks*. These large staffs, modeled after weapons once used by ancient Klingon warriors, are fitted with emitters on each end that deliver powerful, agonizing electrical charges and are used to strike candidates in order to test their courage and strength.

It's definitely not common for offworlders to participate in this particular ritual, although exceptions have been made when a Klingon requests the rite on behalf of a non-Klingon comrade or family member believed deserving of recognition as a warrior in the eyes of the Empire. In the unlikely event you find yourself taking part in this ceremony, here are a few tips to keep in mind:

- Remember and respect the honor you're being shown. Just being here is an acknowledgment that you are worthy to stand alongside true Klingon warriors.
- When you arrive at the columns of waiting warriors, be sure to properly recite your declaration: "Today I am a warrior. I must show you my heart. I travel the River of Blood." It's great if you can say all of this in *tlhIngan Hol*, as that will show those observing the ceremony that you're giving full consideration to the ritual and Klingon customs.
- As you advance through the "gauntlet," stop abreast of each of the four pairs of guards. Stand with confidence. Look straight ahead. Show no weakness.
- It'll only last a moment, but the *painstiks* will definitely hurt. Different physiologies react in varying ways to the incredible shock the weapons inflict, but for most species the sensation is temporary, and there will be no lasting physical damage. Please check with your doctor before participating in the Rite of Ascension.
- After the second and third pairs of warriors administer their *painstiks*, you'll still have lines to speak: "The battle is mine. I crave only the blood of my enemy. The bile of the vanquished flows over my hands."

Only after successfully completing this final challenge can a Klingon warrior truly be accepted by his or her peers.

▲ veS DuSaQ

The ceremonial name for the Klingon military's elite command academy translates to "School of War." Tucked into the foothills east of the city, it is within the confines of this storied institution that the minds and bodies of Klingon warriors are molded. After uncounted generations of secrecy, veS DuSaQ has opened its doors to outsiders so that tourists with an interest in military history and culture can have the chance to witness firsthand some of the most intense, grueling training ever devised. Even though the tour is comprehensive, you'll get only a taste of what candidates endure during their time here. For nearly six months, enrollees are inundated with classroom instruction on numerous topics, including military conduct, skills, protocols, and history. Study is combined with physical training, obstacle and endurance courses, weapons qualification, and armed and unarmed combat. The training, conducted with minimal safety standards, is as brutal as anything a soldier might expect to face on a battlefield or aboard a ship caught in the throes of space combat—a class of one hundred cadets can expect a casualty rate of nearly forty percent. Those who survive this extended trial are rewarded with commissions as officers in the Klingon Defense Force. During tours, interaction between visitors and candidates is strictly prohibited, but instructors and guides are on hand to answer every question. At the end of your tour, you'll share a meal with a cadre of instructors at the academy's mess hall. We recommend avoiding the *klongat* and gravy on toast.

▼ Monument to Kravokh

This striking monument is dedicated to the memory of the chancellor who presided over the Klingon High Council during Krennla's period of transformation into a center of industrial strength during the early twenty-fourth century. The site features an oversized bronze statue of Kravokh standing watch at the center of an expansive botanical garden just south of T'jobhaV Park near the city center. Here, trees and other flora from around Qo'noS are tended with exquisite care, symbolizing the prosperity all Klingons enjoyed under the chancellor's rule, the first stable period of growth and wealth since the loss of the planet's moon, Praxis, in 2293. Unfortunately, several decades later, Kravokh's failure to anticipate a disastrous Romulan attack on the Klingon colony world Narendra III resulted in his removal from power and death at the hands of successor, K'mpec. An unflattering yet accurate recounting of these events can be found on a smaller monument in another section of T'jobhaV Park. Despite his later dishonor, Kravokh's leadership during the planet's most difficult struggles in modern times has earned him continued goodwill, expressed in this modest yet lasting tribute.

SHOPPING AND ENTERTAINMENT

You'll find the vast majority of Krennla's shopping options in the more upscale Baldi'maj District that dominates the city's western half. The affluent residents in this region have discriminating tastes, demanding the best of locally crafted and imported goods. Dedicated cargo shuttles deliver daily shipments of foods and merchandise from the finest and most chic offworld vendors to local merchants. Naturally, you can expect to spend a little extra in this area of the city.

▼ Kas'cA's Market

An unassuming boutique sandwiched between two larger shopping outlets east of the city center, this family-owned store has been in business since Krennla's earliest days and retains the name of the patriarch who established it. Dealing in imported as well as locally crafted goods, the brusque yet helpful staff is always ready to assist you with your selection of jewelry, fragrances, and other gifts from conquered and colonized worlds throughout the Empire. Whether you're looking for the hide of a saber bear to fashion a new winter coat, a bottle of Rir'itaj brandy from Muldor IV or the bulbs from the restorative *vinadi* herb plant that can only be found in the highest reaches of Kang's Summit, chances are Kas'cA's has them. This is also one of the few places on the planet where you can find spices and gemstones from Khitomer, Boreth, Kessik IV, and even Rura Penthe.

▲ *The Ballads of Durall*

The Le'Daqh Theater in the Baldi'maj District's northern end hosts nightly performances of this celebrated Klingon drama. Durall, a legendary warrior who lived during the eleventh century, was said to have ventured across the oceans of Qo'noS to faraway lands on a noble quest assigned to him by the emperor. The ballads chronicle his many adventures, several of which are no doubt heavily embellished—if they even happened at all—as he seeks to retrieve prized items and other artifacts that were lost to time during generations of conflict. On his travels, he encounters a variety of foes, beasts, and creatures of the sea. *The Ballads of Durall* has been a staple of Klingon theater since its initial publication six centuries ago, and translations of this seminal work into other languages have made it popular on planets as diverse as Ferenginar, Bolarus IX, and Cestus III.

¶⊙¶ DINING AND NIGHTLIFE

The people of Krennla work hard, play hard, and eat well. *Very* well. Some of the best food on the planet is found here—everything from elegant multicourse event dining to whatever unidentified slop can be thrown into a mug or bowl. If you leave this city with an empty belly, it's your own fault. Forget eating two- or three-day old *pipius* claw here. Instead, expect to find the freshest catch brought in each day from the prime fishing grounds of the BIQ'a'dung Ocean near the planet's northern pole. The bloodwine offered in several of the restaurants has been fermenting in secret wineries for centuries, and includes thousands of barrels protected from destruction centuries ago during the Hur'q invasion and occupation. The nighttime entertainment options are also in keeping with the city's character. You'll find no shortage of loud taverns, games of chance, demonstrations of fighting prowess or feats of strength, and live music. Yes, that means opera. These are the sorts of things that must be experienced firsthand in order to be fully appreciated. Enjoy!

▲ QaQ nItlh roS

Forget upscale dining. Anchoring the Kenta District's northeast corner, this joint doesn't even offer silverware. Shrug off uncertainty and dig into generous portions of *gagh*, and be sure to get to it while it's still moving. The *garbat* meat—marinated for a week in its own blood before being served—is a house specialty of Hagh'dal, the restaurant's self-appointed "master chef." It's also doused in enough *peppadugh* spice to set off smoke alarms, so you'll probably want to keep the water and ale handy. Lots of it.

▲ Vokar's Targ House

With cafeteria-style service and surly employees behind the counter, one might wonder how this family-owned joint, located west of the veS DuSaQ academy, has stayed in business for more than a century. It's certainly a popular destination for cadets enjoying rare furloughs from their training and looking to escape the academy's no-frills dining facility, but the main reason for the restaurant's success is that the food is simply incredible. Vokar's specializes in one thing: heart of *targ*. Prepared daily and served in portions that spill off the plates flung at you by the line workers, this singular menu item is without peer anywhere in the city. The only thing to drink is bloodwine, and you serve yourself from Vokar's seemingly inexhaustible racks of barrels. Locals come from kilometers around to feast, with lines stretching down the street during peak midday and evening hours. Get here early, because the cooks only prepare what's sold to them by game hunters the prior evening. Once the day's catch is gone, the staff kicks out the diners so they can close up and do it all over again the next day.

▼ Sut HabmoHwI' Sargh

In Federation Standard, "The Iron Horse." One of several restaurants and taverns on the Baldi'maj District's south side specializing primarily in human fare, the Horse offers a full bar and is open around the clock. It's operated by Stahj and Esotoq, a pair of Klingon brothers who've been in business for more than three decades. They do their best to whip up the bland, flavorless blobs of burnt meat that many humans tend to favor. All entrees are made to order without replicators, and the brothers welcome all challenges to their ability to create even the most eccentric Earth delicacy. Chicken-fried steak, haggis, Mongolian stir-fry, chop suey; you name it, the brothers can usually throw it together. In thirty years, they've received only one request that stumped them: shrimp étouffée. Their later attempts to put a Klingon spin on the recipe, substituting *pipius* for the shrimp, also ended in disaster and to this day neither brother will discuss this stain on their culinary honor.

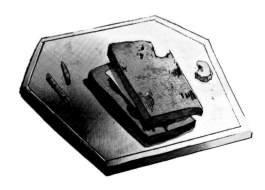

DID YOU KNOW?
APPRECIATING *THE FINAL REFLECTION*

It's easy to forget that some of the most engaging literature of the past several centuries has come to us courtesy of the Klingon Empire. Classics such as *The Dream of the Fire*, *Sto-Vo-Kor Lost*, and *The Ridgeless Warriors* are routinely listed among the most well-known Klingon works. However, when it comes to Klingon-centric novels, many readers are surprised to learn that one of the most celebrated titles in this genre, *The Final Reflection*, was actually written by a human.

A Starfleet officer and cultural anthropologist in the twenty-third century, author J. M. Ford underwent surgery to alter his appearance so that he could pass for a Klingon. He then spent two years living in Krennla with the family of a sympathetic Klingon scientist, Bar'nhaHt, while penning *The Final Reflection*. This seminal work of fiction came about after several unsuccessful attempts to chronicle the actual events surrounding the Babel crisis, a covert military confrontation between the Empire and the Federation. His efforts to uncover the true story thwarted at every turn, Ford instead decided to take what information he had been able to glean and present it as a novel, filtered through the life and experiences of Krenn, a fictional Klingon captain who finds himself caught up in events that threaten to plunge the Empire and the Federation into interstellar war. Ford named his central character in tribute to the city that had been his temporary home.

A best seller when first published on Earth, the novel earned critical praise across the Federation and even notice from within the Empire. More than a century after its original publication, *The Final Reflection* continues to gain new admirers. It's a standard entry on Starfleet's reading list for all officers, and in 2345 it was finally included as part of the curriculum at the veS DuSaQ military academy.

🛏 LODGING

There are plenty of hotels in the city covering a wide selection of price ranges, and most of these establishments—particularly those located in the Kenta District or closer to the city center—offer "nontraditional bedding" for various offworlder physiologies. If you're in town during a commencement ceremony at the veS DuSaQ military academy, rooms at most hotels in the area tend to fill up quickly.

Gejal'toH

One of the first inns to mix traditional decor with a bit of contemporary finesse, the Gejal'toH caters to Klingons and offworlders alike, with rooms on each floor furnished to break with convention. Each of the hotel's ninety-five suites offers a private balcony with a magnificent view of the Baldi'maj District. Take a walk into the hotel's private *na'ran* groves and pick your own bushel of the sweet-tasting, pulpy fruit. While Klingons don't normally enjoy drinking the juice derived from *na'rans*, it is a popular cooking ingredient used to enhance the flavor of *rokeg*-blood pie.

▲ jawbe' chen

Translated as, "Among the Clouds," this hotel holds the distinction of commanding by far the highest point of elevation in the city. It occupies the upper ten floors of the Zabel Tower, which rises 1,800 meters from ground level near the city center, a height more than double that of the tallest surrounding buildings. It was designed and constructed in the early part of the century by Mo'gret, patriarch of the House of IjepoQ, who decided to abandon what he considered the tedious environs of the Baldi'maj District in favor of the more energetic lifestyle to be found downtown. The structure itself is the only one of its kind on the planet, requiring artificial gravity assistance sensors and force fields to hold it steady. Embracing a cosmopolitan flair, the rooms here are extravagantly furnished while still evoking traditional tenets of Klingon culture. Offworlders (and anyone else) who can get past the hotel's unconventional construction will enjoy unrivaled, spectacular views of the city and the regions beyond.

SIDE TRIP: RURA PENTHE

Once known throughout the Galaxy as "the alien's graveyard," Rura Penthe occupies a storied place in Klingon lore. Located in an isolated region of the Empire and well away from Qo'noS, Rura Penthe was considered to be one of the harshest prisons in the Alpha and Beta Quadrants during its period of full operation. When boasting a much larger and more dangerous inmate population during the height of its service, the planetoid was its own best defense against escape attempts. Rugged terrain and subfreezing temperatures on the surface made it inhospitable for all but the hardiest of life-forms. As a result, the prison was located underground.

Efficient and industrious, the prison functioned as a massive slave-labor camp, with inmates working in the planetoid's vast network of subterranean dilithium mines, excavating the valuable ore for use by the Klingon military. Those sent here usually had no hope of parole or reprieve, instead only the grim promise of toiling under bitter working conditions with little chance of long-term survival. When dilithium stores began to decline, most of the prison's population was moved to other facilities, leaving behind only a small cadre of inmates and guards to oversee a reduced, automated mining process. However, as tourism within the Empire began to increase, Rura Penthe's place in Klingon history all but demanded that it be made available to visitors.

If you're visiting from Qo'noS, a tour of Rura Penthe will require at least two full days, including roundtrip transportation to and from the planetoid. All arrivals and departures are conducted via prison personnel transport, though tourists receive far better treatment onboard than inmates would. Be sure you get on the right shuttle.

Transports dock within an underground hangar complex, and, once inside, groups are guided on tours throughout the rest of the facility. Although areas where inmates live and work are strictly off-limits, observation galleries and enclosed connecting walkways afford visitors a unique glimpse into this mysterious inner sanctum. Tour groups move quickly and on a tight schedule, as the facility admits only a limited number of visitors at any one time. The walking tour naturally ends at the prison gift shop, where all of the available knickknacks are handcrafted on-site by the inmate population.

One highlight of the tour is a permanent monument to one of the only prisoners who managed to thwart Rura Penthe's notorious reputation for being escape-proof. Legendary Starfleet captain James T. Kirk, who in 2293 was briefly incarcerated here after being falsely accused of assassinating Chancellor Gorkon of the Klingon High Council, successfully broke out of the subterranean mine and endured the planetoid's unforgiving surface conditions until rescued by his ship, the *U.S.S. Enterprise* NCC-1701-A. As the story of his amazing feat continued to circulate over the years, and the details became increasingly embellished with each retelling, prison officials reluctantly erected the marker and statue at the site of Kirk's escape. The site makes for just one of the numerous holophotographic opportunities you'll find on the walking tour.

Though it lacks anything resembling the sort of amenities you'd expect to find on a typical vacation excursion, there's no denying that Rura Penthe is one of the more interesting stops you'll make during any tour of the Klingon Empire.

KETHA PROVINCE

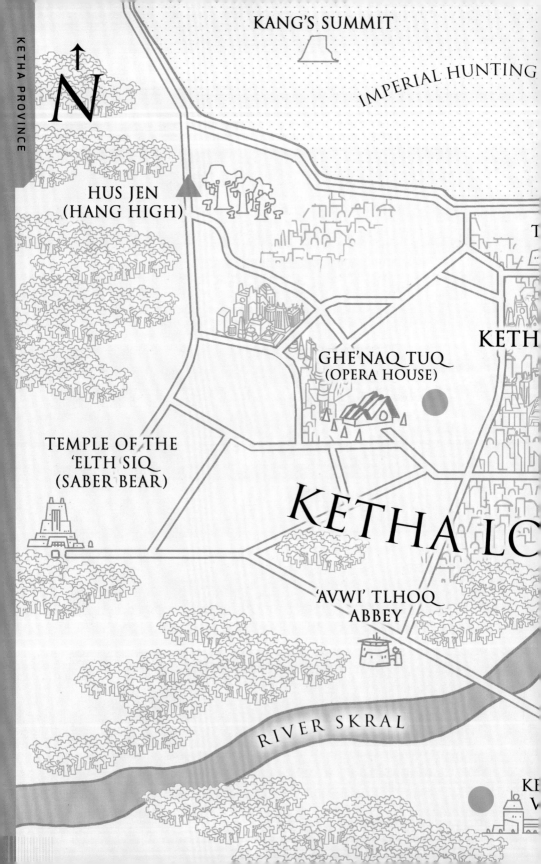

OUNDS

SNAPPED BAT'LETH
★

CITY

PACH HUTLH' PIRMUS
(BOTTOMLESS CLAW)
★

MAQDO'H
GALLERY

WLANDS

LOWLANDS
ORS CENTER

● SHOPPING &
RECREATION

★ DINING &
NIGHTLIFE

▲ LODGING

FAR FROM THE FIRST CITY and some distance inland from the eastern shores of the primary landmass, the Ketha Province is perhaps the best place to see a part of Qo'noS untouched by the hand of progress.

Though the small city of Ketha is a magnet for commerce and visitors, it is the surrounding Ketha Lowlands and the nearby Kintak Jungle that attract legions of enthusiastic big game hunters from across the planet. In addition to the always elusive and dangerous 'etlh SIQ (saber bear), there is also the Ilngta' hunt, held each year on the Imperial Hunting Grounds. An area of the Lowlands normally designated for use by the military and members of the High Council, it is here that Klingon youths undertake their first hunt without adult supervision, stalking the prized Ilngta' beasts while armed only with a spear.

Bordered to the west by the TlhIngtuj Mountains, the region was once hotly contested in the years following the Hur'q invasion—an occupation that led to the looting of most of the planet's natural resources. Ketha remained one of the few areas relatively untouched by the Hur'q's plundering, and several of the more prominent family Houses from the First City saw the potential of mining dilithium and other rare metals and minerals in the region. This helped to establish trade and cargo routes through Ketha Province, linking inland territories to the Chu'paq Sea and the NIHbIQ'a' Ocean to the east. During that period, the Port of Chu'paq that marks Ketha Province's eastern boundary was the primary point of entry for this area, with goods from other cities and provinces transferred to ground transport trains bound for the interior regions. Today, the port continues to serve as a hub for passenger and cargo spacecraft.

GETTING AROUND

A network of mag-rail and conventional overland trains weaves through the province, including the city of Ketha and its outskirts. In Ketha itself, the city streets and footpaths are well-maintained, and walking the central district after dark is an event unto itself thanks to the brilliant lighting and bold, colorful building facades that infuse the otherwise unremarkable streets with a vibrant carnival atmosphere. If you want to take an excursion into the Ketha Lowlands, you'll likely need a Vikak or Sporak all-terrain vehicle, particularly if you're looking to leave the roads and trails. Another option is to take advantage of special tours that utilize anti-gravity suits and allow you to view this expansive wilderness region from the air.

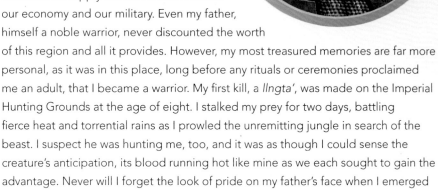

KETHA,
THE EMPIRE'S SALVATION

[First published in the 2377 Edition]
Ketha Province, the place of my birth.
Though perhaps not as ostentatious
as the First City, there is no denying
the region's value to the Empire, as it
continues to supply vital resources that fuel
our economy and our military. Even my father,
himself a noble warrior, never discounted the worth
of this region and all it provides. However, my most treasured memories are far more
personal, as it was in this place, long before any rituals or ceremonies proclaimed
me an adult, that I became a warrior. My first kill, a *IIngta'*, was made on the Imperial
Hunting Grounds at the age of eight. I stalked my prey for two days, battling
fierce heat and torrential rains as I prowled the unremitting jungle in search of the
beast. I suspect he was hunting me, too, and it was as though I could sense the
creature's anticipation, its blood running hot like mine as we each sought to gain the
advantage. Never will I forget the look of pride on my father's face when I emerged
from the jungle, covered in blood and mud and carrying my prize over one shoulder.

As I grew older, I came to understand and appreciate the role the city of Ketha
played, along with the entire province, in helping our people pull themselves from
the brink of annihilation. After we forced the Hur'q from Qo'noS, it was here that
we began the long process of rebuilding our civilization. One of the few areas of
Qo'noS to escape Hur'q devastation, it was the Ketha Province that provided the
seeds of our salvation, allowing our Empire to rise once again.

However, it is the Lowlands that continue to draw me back, and I return as often
as my duties permit so that I might recapture the thrill of those hunts I enjoyed as
a boy. It is also one of my greatest honors to oversee the annual *IIngta'* hunt there,
watching over the next generation of Klingons as they challenge their young minds
and hearts while striving to unlock their true potential as warriors of the Empire.

—**Martok, Chancellor of the High Council**

SIGHTS AND ACTIVITIES

While the city of Ketha offers more options for sightseeing as well as tourist-friendly dining, shopping, and entertainment, the more interesting points for outdoor enthusiasts lie on the province's outskirts and on the borders of the Lowlands. It's here that you'll discover some real local color in ramshackle hunting gear shops and quaint, even charming dive bars and restaurants frequented by hunters and other locals.

Ketha Lowlands Visitors Center

Designed for both Klingons and offworlders, this visitors center is located at the main ranger station just east of the mag-rail terminal along the region's southern boundary. It houses a modest museum that offers a complete history of the area, with special focus on the era that saw settlers arrive from the coastal territories in search of the riches to be found in mining dilithium and other precious ores. There's also an expansive exhibit showcasing the wide variety of animal life to be found in the Lowlands and the Imperial Hunting Grounds. *Targ* and *Ilngta'* are prominently featured of course, and there's also a shrine to the *'etlh SIQ,* or "saber bear," the fiercest and most respected of all the big game predators. Artifacts and recordings recount tales of notable hunts, including numerous instances where the saber bear was the victor.

▲ Anti-Gravity Tours

Without question, the best way to experience the breathtaking beauty of the Ketha Lowlands is from the air. Anti-gravity suits offer adventure seekers an unparalleled view of the region. Following pre-programmed flight paths, they soar to heights averaging fifty meters above the ground. You may even find yourself in an impromptu race with a herd of *targs* who've spotted you from the ground and think you might make for a tasty dinner. Platforms scattered throughout the area afford opportunities for sightseeing and photography, or travelers can pause their suit's flight program and simply hover above the ground.

▲ 'avwl' tlhoQ Abbey

The Klingons who call this monastery home have devoted their lives to the protection of the Lowlands, or the "guarding of nature." To that end, they live deep within the forest, almost at the region's center, and keep watch over the wilderness surrounding them. Rather than discouraging hunting or fishing within the region's lush wilderness, the clerics here foster and promote a greater understanding of the land and the creatures that call it home, so that hunters will have a deeper respect for the prey they stalk. It is one of the paramount tenets of big game hunting on Qo'noS that nothing is wasted; an animal taken from this life must serve noble purpose. Some Klingons believe that before beginning the hunt, the spirit of the prey should be summoned via meditation and its permission sought. Once the animal's spirit concedes, the hunt can begin, but after the hunter succeeds in making the kill, he or she is honor-bound to thank the animal for its sacrifice. In addition, its meat must serve as a hearty repast, and its hide used to provide clothing or shelter. Even its bones can be put to use, fashioned into tools or even jewelry or sculpture. Though the taking of trophies is part of the victory, killing any creature for that sole purpose is considered anathema to the true objective of the hunt. The ritual surrounding this preparation and understanding is known as the *qaD qa'*, or "challenge of spirit."

Rafting on the River Skral

Subterranean springs beneath the Tlhlngtuj mountain range feed this narrow, fast-moving tributary that winds through the Lowlands. Novice rafters will find themselves facing a steep learning curve if they happen to visit after the seasonal thaw, when torrential rains can flood low-lying areas and elevate the river levels. Even those with greater experience will find their skills tested as they navigate the Skral's raging waters. And did we mention the possibility of coming face-to-face with an *'Iw ghargh je*? The enormous and feisty "blood snake" is attracted to the body heat of most humanoid-sized organisms, and there are even reports that the temperamental reptiles have attacked and capsized rafts in the area. River guides are usually trained to deal with the menacing creatures, but if you find yourself in the water with one, dive deep before attempting to swim away, as the *'Iw ghargh je* is unable to hold its breath beneath the surface.

▲ Temple of the *'etlh SIQ*

Located five kilometers from the Lowlands' western boundary, this impressive tribute to the most respected of all big game predators, the saber bear, stands thirty meters tall. The temple appears to be carved out of the rock itself and takes the form of the head and upper torso of a massive saber bear, its front claws raised and poised to strike. The workmanship is exquisite, rivaled only by the life-size bear statue tucked within the stone temple's inner sanctum. No one knows who built this temple, or for what purpose, although glyphs carved into the walls offer some insight into the people who placed this marker, with scans indicating that the temple has stood for nearly 2,400 years—placing it in an era that predates the rule of Kahless. Intriguingly, some historians contend that the carved markings seem to describe the coming of a great leader destined to lead "all people under the sun." Researching and identifying the author of this prophecy, and attempting to learn the source of his apparently divine inspiration, is one of many unsolved mysteries of Klingon history and continues to occupy the monks who live here.

SHOPPING AND ENTERTAINMENT

Like the larger cities, where Klingons are more willing to welcome offworlders, Ketha City has embraced the idea of tourism with great enthusiasm. What's more, its remote location and the access it offers to outdoor pursuits has allowed the city and the surrounding province to offer something unique when competing for the attention of visitors. The city itself offers a wide variety of shopping options, whereas the entertainment venues tend to heavily favor local customs and tastes. If you're an outdoor person, then the villages and shops along the outskirts leading into the Lowlands are where the real action is.

Bat'leth Competitions

Nothing illustrates a Klingon's fighting prowess more than their mastery of the bat'leth, the warrior's traditional bladed weapon. Although the annual interstellar finals tournament, where Klingons pit their bat'leth skills against one another, is held on different worlds each year, the regional qualifying tournaments for Qo'noS take place in the Ketha Lowlands and are open to the public. Bat'leth practitioners of every skill level converge for the grueling competition at the exhibition amphitheater located on the Lowlands' Imperial Hunting Grounds, undertaking as many as eighteen single-elimination challenges over the course of five days. The winners in each category earn the right to represent Qo'noS in the finals, with the winner receiving trophies, accolades, dinner with the Chancellor of the High Council, and bragging rights until next year's competition. Though the tournaments aren't intended to be to the death but are instead presented as sporting contests, accidents do happen on occasion. Visitors and onlookers are encouraged to attend classes and demonstrations that further illuminate the art of fighting with the storied blade.

Maqdo'H Gallery

Located in the retail district within the center of Ketha City, this unassuming shop is stuffed to the rafters with a vast assortment of stone and ceramic sculptures. Though many of these pieces depict figures and animals from Klingon history and mythology, it is the abstract creations unique to the Ketha area, free-flowing and full of color, that seem to attract the attention of visitors. All of the pieces are crafted by Maqdo'H, an artist of some renown who eschewed the distractions and chaos of the First City generations ago by emigrating east for a quieter, more rewarding life. Despite her indeterminate age, Maqdo'H never fails to create at least two new pieces each day, and visitors often watch for hours as she creates a new sculpture, hoping for the chance to buy it.

DID YOU KNOW?
KLINGON OPERA: A FEAST FOR YOUR EARS!

For all the time and effort they devote to war and other martial matters, it's easy to forget that Klingons are also very passionate when it comes to art and music, and, in particular, their operas. For uncounted generations, opera has fueled the imagination and warmed the heart of many a Klingon. One of the earliest examples of the form is *The Battle of Gal-Mok*, a sweeping tale of war and conquest set during the Heroic Age, which has thrilled audiences since its initial performances more than 1,500 years ago. Also hugely popular is *Kahless and Lukara*—which depicts the romance between the first emperor and his equally formidable mate—an opera many regard as the greatest Klingon love story ever told. More recent offerings include *Goqlath Castle* and *The Battle of San-Tarah*, both of which continue the time-honored tradition of translating the history of epic conquests into musical form. Klingon opera thrives in venues around the planet, including the *ghe'naQ tuq* ("opera house") in Ketha, and the only true way to experience it is through live performance. Though Tellarites in particular have no love for the form—many likening it to the throaty mating calls of the *gangual* beasts from their own home planet—other species, including humans, seem to enjoy the evocative themes that dominate most of these Klingon musical epics.

🍴 DINING AND NIGHTLIFE

Several restaurants and taverns within Ketha City offer non-Klingon food options and welcome outsiders with open arms. However, be warned that "quiet dining" is not something you'll find in abundance here. House bands are common, with patrons often encouraged to sing along to the musical accompaniment mid-meal. Thunderous renditions of bawdy drinking songs such as "Bloodwine in My *Gagh*" can rattle the timbers at many a bar and restaurant.

▲ *The Battle at San-Tarah*

The *ghe'naQ tuq* in Ketha City has hosted a performance of this hit opera each night for the past seven years, with nearly every show drawing capacity crowds. For whatever reason, many people tend to think of opera as "old music," not realizing that some of the most celebrated entries in the genre have been composed in the last century. *The Battle at San-Tarah* is one such example. Penned just over a decade ago, this moving story depicts the first Klingon contact with the Children of San-Tarah, a warrior culture that proved to quite be a match for the Empire when a Klingon force, led by Captain Klag of the *IKS Gorkon*, invaded its world. The Children of San-Tarah eventually earned Klag's admiration, and he ultimately used his forces to defend them against a subsequent assault by his own commander, General Talak. Although it's since become one of the most popular shows in cities around the planet, the Ketha *ghe'naQ tuq* is still considered to be the premier venue for experiencing its full grandeur.

The Snapped *Bat'leth*

Owned by Nova'Q, perhaps the oldest Klingon ever to walk the face of Qo'noS, this decrepit bar, situated less than a kilometer from the main entrance to the Imperial Hunting Grounds, has been a favored watering hole for hunters and other outdoor enthusiasts for generations. The food here is simple Klingon fare, but if that's not to your tastes, then Nova'Q might show grudging mercy on you by creating something more palatable using the small replicator tucked behind the bar. A gregarious host, Nova'Q spends each evening patrolling the tables and booths, entertaining patrons with a seemingly inexhaustible supply of anecdotes from his military days that usually have the entire room in stitches. The broken weapon that gives the place its name hangs along the tavern's back wall, a prize taken by Nova'Q from a rival decades earlier during a *bat'leth* competition. According to some of the regular patrons, Nova'Q treasures it more than the trophies he later won, and if you ask nicely, he may well regale you with the tale of how he came to claim his prize. As the evening wears on and the bloodwine starts flowing, expect invitations to participate in a *B'aht Qul* challenge (see page opposite). Accept such offers with caution.

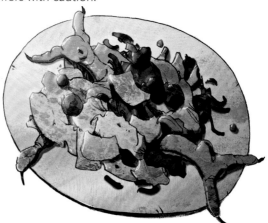

▲ **pach Hutlh pIrmuS**

Loosely translated, the name of this quaint little dive means "bottomless claw." Located inside the rail station terminal on Ketha City's east side, pach Hutlh pIrmuS has a decent menu featuring an impressive range of Klingon cuisine, but many of the regulars come here for the all-you-can-eat *pipius* claw. The appendages from this tentacled sea creature are a delicacy on Qo'noS, and fresh *pipius* is transported each day from fishing ports along the PoSbIQ'a' Ocean. Don't believe those other travel guides; *pipius* tastes absolutely nothing like any domesticated fowl hailing from Earth. When cooked in the mildly intoxicating venom it produces from sacks in its tentacles, the claw meat takes on a mouthwatering, tangy flavor that goes great with a pint of *warnog*. pach Hutlh pIrmuS prepares the claw the proper way: marinated in a thick *grapok* sauce and served bowl after heaping bowl. Antacid tablets are available upon request.

DID YOU KNOW?
THE *B'AHT QUL* CHALLENGE

This test of arm and upper body strength is a popular pastime in many a bar and tavern. Though warriors often engage in the activity as part of their formal training, younger and brasher soldiers like to boast that it's not until you take on all comers at your favorite tavern that you can call yourself a true champion.

For those thinking about accepting such a challenge, it's good to be mindful of the proper protocol. The challenge is a test of simple strength, with the rules calling for you to face your opponent and extend your arms. A referee—usually the bartender in a tavern setting—decides which opponent will place their arms between the other's, crossed at the wrists. If you're the challenger with your arms placed on the inside, your task is attempting to spread your opponent's arms, while they try to push yours together. Once the match begins, you keep going until one of you wins. Victory is declared if you're able to spread your opponent's arms out to their sides, whereas your challenger wins if they are able to force your forearms to touch. The referee's decision is final, with the loser buying the bar a round of drinks. So, don't accept this challenge lightly, as defeat will likely end up being quite expensive.

For those wondering: Breaking, dislocating, or severing a limb constitutes a win (or a loss, if you're the one with a snapped arm).

This exercise is obviously not for the timid, but accepting such an offer as an offworlder might just earn you a bit of respect from the Klingon patrons and perhaps even a free drink or two—assuming you don't require immediate medical attention following the challenge.

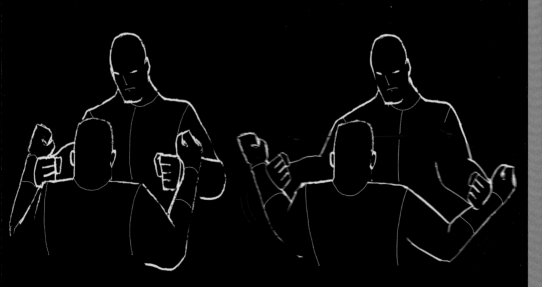

🛏 LODGING

As with most Klingon cities, don't expect lavish accommodations. Here in Ketha City, "fancy" translates to a metal sleeping slab instead of stone. Seasoned travelers know to bring along their own bedding materials when staying in these places, and a few proprietors also rent out padded mats or cushions. Other visitors bypass the hotels altogether and head for the Lowlands, where camping and other rustic lodging options can be found.

▼ HuS jen

One of the most alluring ways to take in the Lowlands is to get as close to the area as possible, and the hotel HuS jen (which translates as "hang high") offers a novel and thrilling way to do just that. Located along the region's western boundary, this elaborate network of tree cottages is a must for travelers who want to experience the raw beauty of the region. Ladders and wooden stairs provide access to these quaint structures that sit as many as forty meters above the ground, connected via wooden catwalks, and afford spectacular views of the wilderness and the distant mountains. Members of hotel staff enter the Lowlands each day to hunt for game, which is later consumed during the nightly *tlho' 'uQ'a'*, or "feast of gratitude," in which staff and guests offer their appreciation for the forest and the animals that have provided such a plentiful banquet. In the morning, be sure to wake up in time to see the sunrise casting a spectrum of brilliant hues across snow-covered peaks and towering trees—it's a sight guaranteed to make your heart skip a beat.

▲ Camping

There's nothing like sleeping under the stars, particularly when you're well away from the lights and other distractions of modern city life. The Ketha Lowlands offer some of the most scenic areas for "getting back to nature" you're liable to find on Qo'noS. Wildlife stewards oversee designated camping sites that are open to tour groups and individuals, and along with being able to hike in with your own provisions, you're also able to fish and hunt in a designated area adjacent to the Imperial Hunting Grounds along the territory's northern edge. Hunting and fishing are also permitted on Kang's Summit and the Tlhlngtuj Mountains even farther to the north. Seasoned guides accompany all hikers and campers, and the protected camping areas are equipped with special hypersonic transmitters that repel local wildlife by emitting a disquieting signal beyond the hearing of most humanoid species. However, be warned that *klongats* are somewhat resistant to the sound. Larger than a *targ*, these notorious quadrupeds hunt at night, employing their razor sharp claws and long, curved fangs with ferocious efficiency. Campers should be aware that *klongats* occasionally stalk the perimeter of the protected areas. Should you encounter one, you should immediately notify your guide, who will be trained to deal with such threats. More often, however, you'll simply hear two or three *klongats* wailing to one another, as their high-pitched calls can carry over great distances.

SIDE TRIP: NARENDRA III

Originally the site of a Klingon colony world, Narendra III and its home system were selected for conquest because of their close vicinity to territory claimed by the Romulan Star Empire. Later, after the Klingons became aware of Earth, the Narendra system took on even greater importance as a point of early detection for possible invasion either by the Romulans or the Federation. The original colony on Narendra III was destroyed in 2344 during a Romulan surprise attack that took the lives of thousands of settlers, but the colony has since been rebuilt and is now more expansive than ever, boasting a population nearly triple that of the original settlement.

Narendra III's distance from the system's binary stars, Narendra A and Narendra B, provides a near perfect balance of climate conditions that make it an idyllic location for colonists and vacationers. Given the Narendra system's close proximity to the Federation-Klingon border, the planet has also become something of an unofficial meeting point for summits between the two interstellar powers. The attack on Narendra III and its aftermath represents one of the pivotal moments in Federation-Klingon relations, and both sides are eager to ensure the planet's significance never fades from historical memory.

GETTING AROUND

Narendra III's habitable landmass is divided among twelve continents of varying size, all of which are accessible via air or watercraft as well as transporters. The primary settlement, Mojatahl, is located in the flatland that lies nearly one hundred kilometers west of the Jo'vrong mountain range that cuts across the center of the planet's largest continent, Hij'ahQ. Smaller villages are scattered across the two next largest landmasses, but only Mojatahl and the area in its immediate vicinity are included in tourist packages, and transport to and from the planet is directed through the central spaceport south of the colony. It's also the only area supported by underground high-speed anti-grav sled conduits, though all of the settlements are reachable via transporter and water or air transportation.

 ## SIGHTS AND ACTIVITIES

The planet's temperate climate means that the beaches and the warm emerald-green ocean waters that encircle most of the Hij'ahQ continent are available for enjoyment year round. The beaches along the northern and southern coastlines are lined with fine powder sand composed of erinadium crystals flushed from rivers and streams running down from the immense Jo'vrong Mountains. Erinadium itself is a valuable mineral ore used for power generation on many Federation and nonaligned worlds, and plans to construct a mining facility are currently under way. If the beaches aren't your thing, there are always city squares and markets in Mojatahl along with the expansive orchards that form the settlement's outer boundaries. You could also venture to the oceanfront village of Chempek along the Hij'ahQ continent's southwestern coast and try your hand at parasailing, or enjoy a day fishing on a charter boat. Though Narendra III is home to a wide variety of sea life, one of its most popular delicacies is the *kijav*, a fish that grows to lengths of more than two meters and has a hide covered with long, thin spikes that secrete a powerful toxin that can cause blistering on most humanoid skin. Another local favorite is the monstrous *bot'yaht*, a species of squid with tentacles that can reach lengths in excess of ten meters. If you think you're brave enough to try catching one of these, most of Chempek's charter boat captains are ready to honor your wishes.

Monument to the Fallen

The Romulan attack on Narendra III was devastating and might well have resulted in greater loss of life if not for the unlikely yet timely intervention of a Starfleet vessel, the *U.S.S. Enterprise* NCC-1701-C. Despite the efforts of the crew of that starship, which also was lost during the battle, thousands of Klingons fell on that fateful day, including children and other noncombatants. Located at the spot west of Mojatahl where the first known casualties fell to Romulan disruptor fire, a towering black granite obelisk inscribed with the names of every victim stands in lasting tribute to those lost on that day. The *chay' 'ej wlj*, or "prayer and reflection," park surrounding the monument is considered sacred ground, and guards posted at the entrances are unforgiving when carrying out their duty to maintain the monument's solemn atmosphere.

DID YOU KNOW?

THE *U.S.S. ENTERPRISE* NCC-1701-C AT NARENDRA III

No discussion of the deceitful attack on this colony can be conducted without acknowledging the role of the Federation and Starfleet in turning back the tide of Romulan aggression against the Klingon Empire. After the attack was launched and the various settlements were under bombardment—first from four Romulan warships in orbit and later by smaller craft engaged in air-to-ground combat runs—colony administrators dispatched a distress call. Though assistance from Klingon warships was on the way, it was obvious to those on the ground that the colony would surely fall before that help could arrive.

What could not be anticipated was the speed and ferocity with which the colony's pleas were answered by another vessel: the *U.S.S. Enterprise* NCC-1701-C.

Commanded by the human Captain Rachel Garrett, the Starfleet warship wasted no time wading into the skirmish. Despite sustaining heavy damage, the *Enterprise* was able to hold off its adversaries long enough that the Romulan ships were compelled to retreat rather than face Klingons in honorable combat. The *Enterprise* was destroyed, with only a handful of the crew surviving.

The courage and sacrifice of Captain Garrett and her crew was a gesture not lost on Klingons, who place honor in combat above all other considerations. This noble act on behalf of the Narendra colonists served to solidify the uneasy alliance that had existed between the Empire and the Federation since the signing of the Khitomer Accords in 2293, eventually leading to the lasting peace the two powers enjoy to this day.

▼ S'tavadag Family *Pe'bot* Farm

One of the largest orchards of its type anywhere in the Empire, this repository for growing *pe'bot*, a succulent local fruit beloved by Klingons, was one of the first areas restored following the attack in 2344, and only began producing its full yield less than a decade ago. Situated along the Mojatahl settlement's northern boundary, the farm is owned and operated by the House of S'tavadag, which tragically lost nine family members during the attack on the colony. Automated tenders cultivate and harvest each season's crop, while members of the S'tavadag family oversee every aspect of the operation, as they have since the colony was first founded. Exports of *pe'bot* to Qo'noS and other Klingon worlds are a significant contributor to the colony's economy, and the orchard itself has become a popular gathering spot for festivals and parties. Tourists

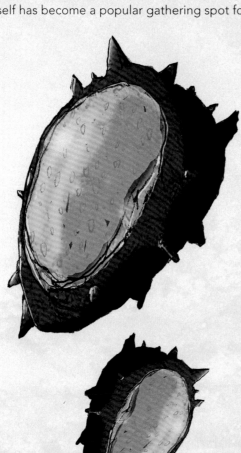

are encouraged to visit the farm and venture into the fields to make their own selections—but be wary: You won't be able to eat just one! Sweet and pulpy, *pe'bot* are adaptable to any number of recipes, and you'll have a chance to sample a large number of culinary creations during your visit, courtesy of the farm's delectable kitchen. *Pe'bot* tarts are a favorite children's treat, and the juice of the fruit can also by used by talented chefs to enhance the taste of everything from *rokeg*-blood pie to several varieties of *gagh* worms.

▼ Narendra III Colonial Museum

This museum, dedicated to the Romulan attack and its aftermath, is located in the Mojatahl colony's eastern quarter. It charts a full history of the settlement, the events leading up to that tragic day, and, of course, an extensive exploration of the attack itself, highlighted by recorded interviews from survivors and other witnesses. The museum is also host to a special annex of the Hall of Honor on Qo'noS, containing a permanent exhibit on the *U.S.S. Enterprise* NCC-1701-C and the role it played in the battle, commemorating the sacrifice of Captain Rachel Garrett and her crew and examining the subsequent shift in the Empire's relations with the Federation. The museum is built atop a small plateau where its great glass dome catches the rays of the morning sun and redirects them to illuminate the tomb of K'pec'Ja, the leader of the colony's security contingent who perished on the day of the attack while defending civilians from the Romulan onslaught. Using only a disruptor rifle from the outpost's small armory, K'pec'Ja disabled four Romulan assault craft and led a group of eighteen settlers to safety before being mortally wounded. He was posthumously awarded the Order of the *Bat'leth* by Chancellor Kravokh and interred here, so that the story of his courage and sacrifice will be remembered forever.

🛍 SHOPPING AND ENTERTAINMENT

While initially reluctant to embrace tourism, the locals have recently been warming to the idea as the tragic history of the colony continues to resonate within the Empire and the Federation, driving a steady stream of visitors to the area. A small assortment of shops can be found scattered around the colony, but Mojatahl has no major retail center. Other merchants simply operate boutiques from their homes or farms. The colonists prefer this approach as it allows them greater opportunity to showcase the local creative talent, in everything from foodstuffs to candles, clothing, art, and sculpture.

▼ Sleeping *Klongat* Curio Shop

A statue of a giant slumbering *klongat* cast in gold sits next to this dilapidated disaster shelter turned general store. South of Mojatahl and positioned for maximum effect just outside the spaceport hub where charter transports arrive and depart, the Sleeping Klongat stands ready to provide travelers with the sort of must-have items that are always forgotten during a vacation. Lha'drel, the retired farmer who owns the decrepit structure, is one of the few remaining survivors of the Romulan attack. If you ask respectfully, he'll regale you with tales of heroism and tragedy from that day and the years afterward. Enjoy the stories, but keep an eye on your watch, or else you're liable to become so engrossed that you miss your ride back to Qo'noS.

🍽 DINING

While there are a few culinary options to choose from, remember that the majority of the vendors here are still working toward being able to cater to the increasing number of tourists in their midst. As such, the fare will largely be to the likings of the locals, which means it'll crawl off its plate and point you back to your charter transport if you're rude about the menu.

▼ K'vaad's Eatery

Situated near Mojatahl's *veng Suvwl' botlh,* or "town center," this open-air restaurant is a favorite of colonists and is also one of the few establishments that caters to offworlder tastes. A replicator is on hand to fulfill non-Klingon dietary requirements, but if you're looking to try something daring, then you can't leave without sampling the *ri'yatla* liver. Taken from one of the planet's larger game animals, this local delicacy is prepared by dousing it in a thick, spicy sauce known locally as *qul nlm tlhagh* or "fire butter," which, according to one of our reviewers, tastes like it may have been extracted from the planet's molten core. Tread carefully.

🛏 LODGING

There are a handful of inns and lodges scattered around the main settlement, but those are limited as the colony's infrastructure isn't presently able to accommodate large numbers of outsiders. However, community leaders have seen the advantage of providing for longer stays by offworlders, and plans are afoot to expand the planet's tourist accommodations as part of ongoing expansion efforts.

Sol'taj Rocks

Look closely and you'll see that this quaint collection of bungalows overlooking the Sol'taj River, east of Mojatahl, is actually built on the remains of an emergency disaster relief camp, hastily erected in the days following the Romulan attack. Over time, the temporary housing shelters were replaced with more permanent structures as reconstruction efforts continued. Fed from waterfalls in the foothills of the Jo'vrong Mountains to the northeast, a fast-moving river runs through the area, cascading over large boulders littering the riverbed to create a series of challenging rapids that many choose to brave during the summer rafting season. A footbridge across the water will take you to the Monument to the Fallen, which, at night, looms like a dark, silent sentry above the trees lining the river.

HOW TO TALK TO KLINGONS (WITHOUT INSULTING THEM)

Despite a reputation for being incredibly complex, in reality Klingon etiquette is rather straightforward and can be summarized by a simple axiom: Don't insult a Klingon or a Klingon's honor. What can make it tricky to abide by this rule are the sheer number of rituals and traditions that permeate Klingon culture. It's therefore essential to familiarize yourself with such things before venturing into the Empire for your holiday excursion.

For example, Klingons respect strength and self-assurance, so don't step back if a Klingon encroaches upon your personal space. Stand your ground, look directly at the Klingon you're addressing, and speak in a bold, confident voice. This communicates that you are not offended by their proximity. Respond to insults not by questioning a Klingon's opinion, but instead by offering your own observation about that Klingon. For example, if a Klingon steps up to you and informs you that you possess the warrior might of an insect, observe that they smell like the stable of an unwashed *targ*. As often as not, the response you'll receive will be raucous laughter at having passed their little test and an invitation to share a drink.

It's not just talk when it comes to dealing with a Klingon, either. There might even be instances during encounters of this sort where striking the other party is not only a viable option, but necessary. If a Klingon questions your honor or courage, it's entirely acceptable to hit that person across the face. This demonstrates that you do possess your own personal honor and are therefore worthy of respect. However, there is, of course, room for misjudgment. When defending your honor in this way, do so with your fist, rather than an open hand. The former will gain you the genuine respect of the other party, while the latter signals that you find the person contemptible and are now challenging them to a battle to the death. We definitely recommend the first option.

Although violent confrontations between Klingons and hapless visitors were a much larger problem in years past, with the recent increase in tourism, most Klingons are learning to be more accepting of travelers who may not always be aware of the myriad and seemingly contradictory nuances of Klingon culture. This, along with outsiders' increased awareness of Klingon customs and courtesies, has helped to alleviate the regularity of such occurrences. What you are more likely to encounter is locals amusing themselves by pretending to be offended by your bad Klingon language skills just to see the panic in your face. In all such situations, be bold, aggressive, and ready to run like a saber bear if the Klingon produces a *d'k tahg* knife.

QUIN'LAT

HUD' MACH
MOUNTAINS

THREE T
BRID

GREAT DOMES
OF QO'NOS

QU

MIVDAQ JONLU'CH
(GO'DAHL' PARLO

QUIN'LAT
PLAZA

(ORI

NGENG
RETLHDAQ
(BY THE SEA)

PO
TEA

POSBIQ'A' OCEAN

MIN'AQ
THEATER

JIN

MUSEUM OF
MILITARY TRIUMPH
AND CONQUEST

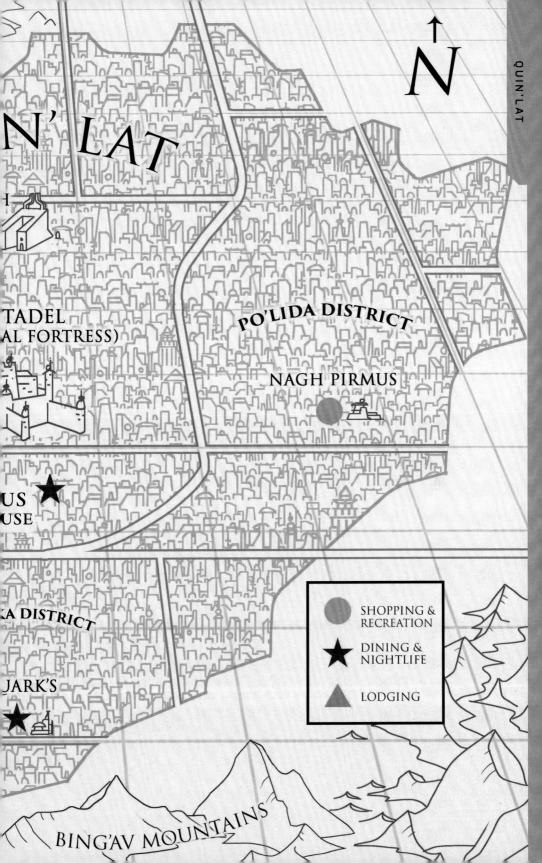

N

N' LAT

TADEL
AL FORTRESS)

PO'LIDA DISTRICT

NAGH PIRMUS

US
USE

A DISTRICT

JARK'S

SHOPPING &
RECREATION

DINING &
NIGHTLIFE

LODGING

BING'AV MOUNTAINS

LOCATED IN THE SUPERCONTINENT'S southern region and inland from the western shores facing the PoSblQ'a' Ocean, Quin'lat forms the southern boundary of the Qo'noS primary trade corridor that was established more than a thousand years ago. That route links this modestly sized metropolis to the First City, as well as destinations scattered across the continent.

The area was first claimed in the ninth century by Emperor Kaldon, who ordered the construction of a military fortress to provide protection for the deepwater port to the southwest and the access points north toward the First City. The original Quin'lat Citadel was a massive undertaking, with a ten-meter high stone wall encircling a compound that could house two thousand soldiers. Lookouts and long-range observation outposts served as satellites for the citadel, providing early warnings of potential invasion by sea or from the plains and mountains to the north and east.

After the renegade dictator, Me'droq, seized control of the citadel, as well as a nearby network of small villages and a monastery to the north known as the Great Domes of Qo'noS, Kaldon ordered a massive sea and land campaign to take them back. The unconventional tactics employed by Kaldon's generals and the armies they commanded resulted in an early victory for the Empire and the total defeat of Me'droq, whom Kaldon later killed with his own *d'k tahg* blade. After the citadel and the surrounding region were reclaimed by imperial troops, the Klingon Empire made a firm commitment to ensuring it stayed out of the hands of marauders like Me'droq, and with investment in its defenses came the expansion and evolution of the scattered villages into a single city, Quin'lat.

Today, Quin'lat serves as the epicenter for the Klingon military industrial complex on Qo'noS, with most of its economy driven by the presence of dozens of factories and hundreds of warehouses that surround the city. Thousands of civilian employees and military personnel are concentrated here, manufacturing a broad spectrum of vital components for the Klingon Defense Force's fleet of warships before they're transported to orbital dockyards around the planet, or other space-based shipbuilding and repair facilities throughout the Empire. The city itself is a mix of architectural styles and infrastructure spanning more than six centuries. Ancient stone structures stand alongside modern buildings, and a conscious effort has been made to preserve as much of the original construction as possible. The most challenging aspect of this endeavor is the original citadel, which has begun to succumb to the ravages of time. A renewed push for restoring the historically significant bastion is currently under way.

 GETTING AROUND

Like most midsize cities on Qo'noS, Quin'lat possesses a reliable, if not stellar, mass-transit system, along with several options for securing privately chartered ground and air vehicles. With a network of transporter hubs and an anti-grav rail system also available, getting to any of the city's major boroughs and landmarks is relatively easy. Aerial tours of Quin'lat offer the most picturesque way to appreciate the range of architectural styles on display in the city. Public transportation will get you to the grounds on which the original citadel stands, but you'll have to walk the structure itself, as modern conveyances are not permitted inside the ancient fortress's stone wall perimeter.

QUIN'LAT: A TURNING POINT FOR THE EMPIRE

[First published in the 2295 Edition]

The importance of Quin'lat cannot be understated. I admit to personal bias, as the city is the place of my birth, and I still return here whenever my duties permit. However, there is no denying that the city's role in Klingon history is one of distinction. It is a pivotal location that served to bring into sharp focus the Empire's early struggles to unite the Klingon people, as personified by the conflict between Emperor Kaldon and one of his most storied nemeses, Me'droq.

Following his victory over his would-be rival, Kaldon set into motion a grand scheme to return Quin'lat to its former glory. Befitting its place in our history, the city was expanded in size as well as influence, a process that continued for centuries as Quin'lat became a nucleus for trade and commerce as well as the heart of the Klingon military machine. Every Klingon who has commanded a warship to victory has done so in a vessel constructed from components forged here, each crafted with the same dedication that any soldier would give to constructing their own personal weapon. In times of strife and great challenge, the men and women of this city have given their all toward furthering the security of all Klingon people.

Founded not through conquest but instead upon the simple principle of expansion and security for a people striving for unity, Quin'lat was and remains an anchor point not just in the beginning of our civilization but also in our future prosperity.

—Azetbur, Chancellor of the High Council

SIGHTS AND ACTIVITIES

For the most part, Quin'lat has plenty to see and do, and many of the most intriguing points of interest naturally revolve around the city's origins and history. The exhibits and landmarks you'll find here paint an accurate, if sometimes unpleasant, picture of the events that provide Quin'lat with its indelible mark on Klingon history. Most of the city's outlying areas—specifically the military facilities and factories—are off-limits to visitors. The military production plants are active around the clock, so expect congestion during peak travel times as workers move to and from these areas via mass transit.

▼ Quin'lat Citadel

At the very core of the city rests the original fortress, which marks the Empire's initial footprint in the region. Much like the Alamo and the Flavian Amphitheater from Earth's ancient history, or the small military outpost around which the city of ShiKahr was constructed on Vulcan, the citadel stands alone, defying the modern architecture and technology that have encroached up to the very threshold of the castle's ancient fortifications. To a casual observer, the archaic buttresses and the enclosure they protect are an anachronism at the heart of a modern, thriving metropolis. Inside the citadel's courtyard, visitors will find restored battlements that house some of the original cannons and catapults from an age before handheld projectile and energy weapons. An honor guard permanently assigned to the bastion represents the longest-serving military division on the planet. Its responsibilities include attending to the structure itself, as well as the timeworn implements of war it contains. It also carries out morning and evening ceremonial flag processions. If their duties permit, every member of the guard unit is authorized to conduct a guided tour of the fortress and offer insight and stories about the castle and the battles to which it bore silent witness.

▼ Museum of Military Triumph and Conquest

Located on the city's southern outskirts, this museum is an evolving monument to the innumerable warriors who have fought and died in service to the Empire, as well as the battles they won and lost. Housed within a modernized reliquary that was originally built during Emperor Kaldon's reign nearly 1,500 years ago, the museum spans seven chambers filled with exhibits and artifacts, including thousands of pieces seized following Klingon conquests across the quadrant. Many noteworthy battles are chronicled here, along with information on enhancements in warfare technology and tactics, and invaluable accounts from participants on all sides of the conflicts. Not only is the museum the first repository to provide a complete account of the evolution of Klingon warfare, it also holds the distinction of being the first such institution recognized by the High Council as bearing major historical and cultural significance. To that end, the museum receives considerable financial and governmental support aimed at ensuring the conservation and increased public availability of its ever-growing storehouse of artifacts and documents. In addition to the exhibits themselves, visitors can observe Klingon preservation technicians as they work to refurbish or repair various artifacts. Everything from thousand-year-old *bat'leth* and armor to Jem'Hadar fighter craft seized during the Dominion war are brought here for restoration.

▲ Three Turn Bridge

Located north of Quin'lat on the way to the First City, the bridge spans a gap between two small atolls at the tail end of the minor HuD'mach mountain range, offering a spectacular view of the YIjatlhQo' ngech Valley. On a clear day, you can also see the outskirts of the First City. According to Klingon mythology, it was here that Kahless the Unforgettable placed himself between the capital and the army poised to invade it. Sworn to protect his home in the name of the budding Klingon Empire, Kahless stood alone at the midpoint of the mighty bridge, wielding the *bat'leth* he had forged with his own hands and vowing that no enemy would pass. Accounts vary from retelling to retelling, but all claim that no less than five thousand enemy soldiers fell that day, victims either of the emperor's blade or his bare hands. There's no way of confirming that number, or whether the epic battle even took place, but all agree that it's an enthralling story, as evidenced by the hundreds of thousands of Klingons and offworlders that visit the bridge each year. Constructed from the wood of the mighty, indomitable *SIHbe' Sor* tree, the bridge stands unbowed against the ravages of time.

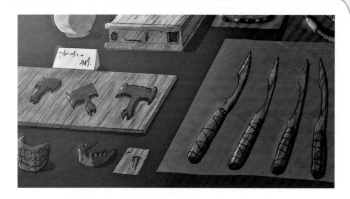

DID YOU KNOW?

THE ENDURING APPEAL OF *BATTLECRUISER VENGEANCE*

Though the idea of Klingons partaking in leisurely pursuits such as the arts, games, or even the viewing of recorded entertainment programs might seem odd to the uninformed traveler, the truth is that this race of proud warriors, like all intelligent species, has its hobbies and pastimes. This definitely extends into the world of entertainment, including books and recorded audio and visual media. Some of these *mIywI' chu' ghun,* or "entertainment and leisure programs," attract followers and fanatics of such devotion that what often begins as an amusing distraction takes on a life of its own, eventually fusing itself within a society's collective consciousness. One such example is *Battlecruiser Vengeance.*

Created as a serial melodrama program in the early twenty-third century, *Battlecruiser Vengeance* is the tale of Captain Koth, the heroic commander of the *Vengeance* who is descended from Emperor Kaldon himself. Born in the Quin'lat region, Koth seeks his destiny among the stars to fight against all enemies of the Empire. The stories, though simple, are essentially parables espousing the values of Klingon honor and courage always triumphing over evil. Despite ceasing production in the mid-twenty-third century, the program continues to attract new generations of followers, and festivals honoring Quin'lat as the birthplace of the fictional ship's commander are held in the city each year. Many Klingons point to its uplifting stories and positive outlook on imperial conquest as one of the main factors in its continuing appeal.

Numerous sequel stories were later produced in novel and holonovel form, and there are now plans to create a new version of the program, set in the modern day with a new, larger *Battlecruiser Vengeance* continuing the fight against the Empire's foes. The series has even extended its influence beyond the Empire's borders and become popular on several Federation worlds. Starfleet officers in particular are always on the lookout for merchandise tied to the program, the best of which is available only within the Empire's borders. So don't be surprised if a friend asks you to pick up a copy of the original recordings or some other *Battlecruiser Vengeance* knickknack during your visit to Quin'lat.

Great Domes of Qo'noS

Situated in the plains due north of the city, this revered landmark has for centuries resisted the ravages of time. To many, the great sandstone domes, which have stood defiant in the face of invasion and oppression, symbolize all that it means to be Klingon. The magnificent structures were built to serve as a monastery, but were later captured by forces loyal to the tyrant Me'droq. Subsequently, the entire structure underwent significant renovations to outfit it as the leader's personal manor. From the Great Domes, Me'droq planned to deploy his legions north and east toward the First City and Qam-Chee, attempting to split territory along the trade route connecting the continent's northern and southern regions. His campaign was cut short when Emperor Kaldon, in a bid to rescue the isolated Quin'lat villagers, dispatched forces north from the BIQ'a'blng Ocean toward the BIng'av Mountains, flanking Me'droq's army before it could reach Qam-Chee. After forcing Me'droq to abandon the Great Domes, Kaldon returned the area to the ousted clerics and placed it under eternal imperial protection. To this day, 1,500 years after that decisive victory, a garrison of Klingon soldiers is permanently assigned here. The Domes contain one of the largest libraries on the planet, including handwritten editions of famous texts by each of the early emperors.

 SHOPPING AND ENTERTAINMENT

Though options aren't quite as diverse as you'd expect to find in one of the larger cities, shopping in Quin'lat can still be fun. There is a broad selection of retail and curio shops, the latter specializing in the sort of souvenirs and other oddities that so characterize shopping in tourist-friendly areas. There are also quite a few art galleries, and musicians and other performers occupy space on various street corners in the Po'liDa entertainment district on the city's east side. Don't miss the Klingon who juggles two *bat'leths* and a *d'k tahg* knife. Although he's quite talented, look closely and you'll see he's missing two fingers from each hand.

nagh plrmuS

If there's a gem and jewelry retailer anywhere else on the planet that can beat this place's rock-bottom prices, we've yet to find it. This quaint little store, located in the middle of the Po'liDa district, features jewelry and other items fashioned exclusively out of rock and mineral deposits taken from the Kri'stak Volcano. The store's owners craft everything by hand, from setting gemstones to fashioning the rocks into a range of custom shapes. Forget the souvenirs everybody else buys. Pick up one or two of these inimitable creations for someone special back home.

▲ *Khamlet*

You've heard the stories and the rumors; now put all remaining doubts to rest as you take in this award-winning adaptation of *The Tragedy of Hamlet, Prince of Denmark*, the play by the famed Earth playwright William Shakespeare. The Min'aq Theater in the city's southern Jin'tika district brings audiences the classic, influential tragedy in "the original Klingon." Though the Empire has known about Shakespeare for at least a century, accounts differ regarding how the Bard's writings found their way to Qo'noS. There are some who believe that this awareness did not come until after a lasting peace was struck with the Federation and cultural information was exchanged. However, some theories claim that Klingon appreciation for *Hamlet* came after an incident in the twenty-second century when a Klingon crashed on Earth and accidentally initiated first contact with humans. As the story goes, the lone pilot, Klaang, became exposed to human literature during his brief time on Earth and later brought the plays of Shakespeare back to Qo'noS. These wildly entertaining yet implausible tales have never been substantiated, and Klaang denied their veracity for the remainder of his days. As for this adaptation, this hearty Klingon production by the superlative actors of the 'angghal Theater Company pulls out all the stops to provide an authentic performance of the noted play, and even though all of the dialogue is rendered in *tlhIngan Hol* and many of the cultural references have been changed to reflect Klingon society and history, you'll soon forget as you're drawn into the experience. With the success of *Khamlet*, the troupe is now working on its next offering, a production of *vIHtaHbogh pagh ado mamej*—a translation of Shakespeare's *Much Ado About Nothing*—which is scheduled to open next year.

DID YOU KNOW?
THE DAY OF HONOR

Another key aspect of Klingon life and culture is the warrior's periodic need for self-reflection, an activity surrounded by its own rituals and traditions. The demands placed on soldiers of the Empire, the rigid discipline by which they must abide, and the responsibilities they carry as representatives of a martial caste dating back centuries are enormous. These duties can often cloud a warrior's mind from the perspective needed to maintain one's honor and display courage in the face of battle.

Therefore, there is a designated day each year when duty requires that all Klingons pause from the rigors of daily life, evaluate their accomplishments, successes, and failures, and determine for themselves whether the actions they've taken are honorable. This ritual observance is known as the *Batlh jaj*, or the "Day of Honor." Though originally intended as an observance only for those officially recognized as warriors of the Empire, the tradition has evolved over time so that nearly all Klingons, military and civilian alike, partake of the ritual. In Quin'lat, festivities are normally observed outside the original citadel, as it is here that the tradition is believed to have been born during the final years of Emperor Kaldon's reign.

During this period of deep contemplation and introspection, each Klingon is required to respect the personal honor of friends and enemies alike. They are also required to treat everyone, regardless of their species or heritage, like a Klingon. As a consequence, anyone—including non-Klingons—can be invited to participate in the Day of Honor and its pivotal ceremonial combat performance known as *suv'batleth*. Following the ritual combat, participants often partake of a feast of fresh *rokeg*-blood pie as a way of closing out the Day of Honor observances.

🍴 DINING AND NIGHTLIFE

There are plenty of food options in the city, and several restaurants cater to non-Klingons. Quin'lat is actually one of the first cities on the planet to make significant strides in this area, and travel experts predict that this effort will one day make this a premier tourist destination.

▲ mIvDaq jonlu'chugh

The name of this lively combination tavern and *Go'daHI'* parlor translates as "seize your fortune." Standing alone five kilometers north of the city on the way to Three Turn Bridge, this ramshackle structure is decorated with enough neon lighting that it's visible from twice that distance, and perhaps even from orbit. The game of *Go'daHI'*, played with an assortment of intricately decorated and colored cards, is at times reminiscent of Earth poker. Anyone is invited to have a seat at the table, though the regular players take the games and the stakes seriously, so don't enter if you don't have the credits to cover your bets.

▲ por SuS Tea House

While it's fair to say that Klingons love their bloodwine, *warnog* and other ales, as well as their coffee, it's also true that they're pretty serious about their tea. The proprietor of the por SuS Tea House, Ra'tijik, has capitalized on that passion with this unassuming little cafe she opened after immigrating to Quin'lat from Ketha Province. The leaves she uses to blend each of her fourteen varieties of herbal teas are all grown in the hydroponics dome she constructed behind her building, which is located south of the original 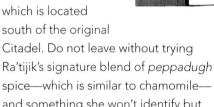 Citadel. Do not leave without trying Ra'tijik's signature blend of *peppadugh* spice—which is similar to chamomile—and something she won't identify but that we think tastes like eucalyptus. Her cafe also offers a small section of *Jlnjoq* breads and toasts. Don't be surprised to see two old Klingons playing *Klin zha* in the cafe's far corner. By all accounts, they've been there, playing the same game, since before Praxis exploded.

Quark's Bar, Grill, Gaming House, and Holosuite Arcade, Quin'lat

Despite the success this franchise has enjoyed on other worlds, Quark's still seems at first to be wildly out of place here on Qo'noS, particularly as it sits tucked among more traditional establishments in the Jin'tika district on the city's south side. Pa'vanoQ, the bar's Klingon manager, was apparently quite taken with the original club during a visit to Federation station Deep Space 9, and lobbied for the opportunity to bring the brand to his home city. Though Pa'vanoQ did import some of the same food and drink selections that made Quark's famous, the menu here favors Klingon cuisine, which, of course, includes beverages fit for a warrior's palate. The holosuites are a popular draw, though most locals prefer the gaming parlor and friendly bouts of *In'zanS* darts or *Wo'dagh*, a card game similar to Pyramid or five-card stud. If you're feeling particularly daring, take Pa'vanoQ's "Fire Breath" challenge, where patrons attempt to eat thirty helpings of *taknar* gizzard in under two minutes. Each of the gizzards is doused in the manager's signature *loppak* hot sauce, making the challenge particularly grueling. Winners earn bragging rights and two free goblets of *warnog*, which go a long way toward soothing your abused taste buds.

🛏 LODGING

Accommodations are abundant in the city, and many of the hotels and inns cater to offworlders. Though the notion of corporate franchise resorts and other such large concept hotels has yet to cement its foothold on Qo'noS, a few larger chains are already developing expansion plans.

▲ Quin'lat Plaza

The first large-scale hotel established on the planet by an offworld corporation, the Plaza welcomes Klingons and outsiders alike. Its location, near the original citadel at the center of the city, places it within easy walking distance of several dining and shopping options. Constructed as a massive, multistory wheel, the hotel is capped by a transparasteel dome, enclosing an artificial waterfall that drops into a huge swimming pool so enticing that even Klingons, who tend to shun water activities, have been known to take a dip. Water warmed by geothermal vents leading from a one-third scale replica of the Kri'stak Volcano keeps the temperature inside the enclosure mild year round. The re-creation is so uncanny that you half expect Kahless to wander into the enclosure and attempt to forge a *bat'leth* from its synthetic lava. Enjoy the hotel's long list of amenities and allow the attentive staff to tend to your every need.

▼ ngeng retlhDaq

Simply put, the title of this modern hotel translates as "By the Sea." Situated away from the more populated areas and overlooking the cove that leads out to the PoSbIQ'a' Ocean, ngeng retlhDaq offers a respite from the faster pace of city life. In addition to the main tower that holds the bulk of the hotel's guest rooms, there are also two-dozen cottages along the water's edge. If you're willing to brave the cold waters of the nearby ocean, you can sign up for special swimming lessons as well as the chance to swim with a school of *okru*, gentle whale-like creatures who have no interest in eating anything besides the enormous amounts of *jus'laQ* shellfish they consume each day. Unlike similar life forms from Earth, *okru* are not air breathers but instead true creatures of the deep. Klingon scientists and Federation xenoichthyologists have recently taken to studying these magnificent creatures, attempting to determine the feasibility of okru being adaptable—via natural or artificial means—to other planets where similar species are endangered, in the hopes of boosting the cetacean population on those worlds. Though they're capable of descending to depths in excess of two thousand meters, *okru* tend to favor the coral reefs just offshore, which are as breathtaking as the whales themselves.

SIDE TRIP: BORETH

Other than Qo'noS itself, there are few planets within the Klingon Empire that are the focal points of so many stories, myths, prophecies, traditions, and rituals as Boreth.

During his legendary declaration that one day he would return from death in order to once more lead the Klingon people, Kahless raised his hand toward the night sky and pointed at a single star, which he claimed would be the location of his return. Centuries later, Klingon warships were dispatched to locate that star, where they found the planet Boreth and a small, pre-industrial humanoid civilization, the Jinvana. Numbering fewer than one million life-forms and possessing nothing in the way of modern technology or weaponry, the Jinvana could offer no resistance to the armada of Klingon warships that arrived and claimed Boreth for the Empire. Upon establishing an occupation army, the Klingon military forced the Jinvana into slave labor camps. Most of the indigenous population was put to work extracting dilithium and other precious ores from beneath the planet's surface.

After geological surveys unearthed a network of lava caves beneath what was later named the SIQ'jlung mountain range, this location was selected for building what became the Boreth Monastery. Jinvana slave labor was used to construct the massive shrine atop the range's tallest mountain peak.

With the monastery completed, clerics, monks, and other Klingons of deep faith from across Qo'noS traveled to the planet, where they took up the cause of awaiting Kahless's return. The clerics who came to live in the monastery requested the removal of the military occupation force and granted the Jinvana their freedom, allowing them to return to their own communities elsewhere around the planet. Some of the Jinvana accepted offers to work at the monastery, and their descendants continue to work there to this day.

Many Klingons make the pilgrimage to visit the monastery and the surrounding grounds, though the rest of this small planet—including those areas which have been returned to the nearly two million Jinvana who are still alive and apparently happy living under Klingon rule—has been declared off-limits on order of the High Council.

While the clerics prefer to keep to themselves, in recent years they have become more accommodating to the presence of non-Klingons following the Empire's efforts to strengthen its ties to the Federation and other unaligned worlds. The clerics and other monastery staff do their best to support the ever-increasing wave of tourism, while maintaining their ceaseless vigil.

 GETTING AROUND

Offworlders aren't allowed to visit the Jinvana communities, but tours of the Boreth monastery are available throughout the planet's solar year, except during specific holidays such as the Muar'tek and Kot'baval festivals. Travelers are advised that winters on Boreth can be brutal, given the monastery's location high in the SIQ'jlung Mountains, but the warmer months make life here quite pleasant. Chartered transports from Qo'noS and other approved departure points within imperial borders arrive and depart at twelve-hour intervals. The monastery is only able to accommodate a limited number of tourists each day, and except for limited guest billet space, there are no lodging options for visitors. Once here, travelers are encouraged to tour the grounds on foot. Be prepared to spend the majority of the day walking between points of interest.

SIGHTS AND ACTIVITIES

The monastery is obviously the big draw here. After more than one thousand years, the clerics who've watched over this shrine have amassed a number of mementos, letters, gifts, and other artifacts given to them by Klingons throughout the Empire as a way of showing devotion to Kahless. Upon receipt, the clerics catalog each item and take steps to ensure its preservation until such time as the first emperor chooses to return. As a result, this repository of offerings has become something of a museum in its own right. Even following the creation of Kahless's clone in 2369, the monastery's caretakers continue to receive a steady stream of donations, which they painstakingly safeguard. Visitors can quickly find themselves lost among the archives, essentially taking a walk through centuries of accumulated history as they discover how Klingons throughout the ages have paid respect to the founder of their civilization.

▲ **Lu!lgh**

Translated as "refuge" or "sanctuary," the monastery's primary shrine is located at the top of the temple's tallest tower. A shaft in the center of the ceiling draws sunlight into the room and illuminates the raised dais, with its array of ornamental candles and a large portrait of Kahless serving as a backdrop. Before the painting is a throne, constructed centuries ago, which now sits empty—waiting for Kahless, the one warrior deemed worthy enough to occupy it. Aside from the clerics themselves, many Klingons of deep faith come here to meditate and draw strength and courage from the essence of the First Emperor that many believe permeates the shrine.

Boreth Botanical Gardens

In addition to the fruits and vegetables grown by the clerics and a small cadre of Jinvana farmers on the monastery grounds, a great deal of time and effort is devoted to nurturing a truly spectacular assemblage of flora from around Boreth as well as from Qo'noS and other Klingon-occupied worlds. Walking paths and rivers winding through the trees serve as buffers between incompatible species, including one genus of predatory plant that can actually launch small stingers from its stigma, each teeming with a nerve toxin that is quickly fatal to many humanoids. In true Klingon fashion, the plants are not segregated or enclosed, meaning the clerics take their lives into their own hands when it's time to tend the gardens. Warning signs are posted and medical treatment is available in case of emergency, of course, and visitors are advised to exercise extreme caution when venturing to this area of the grounds.

Spires of Boreth

A natural rock formation that's visible from the observation deck on the monastery's uppermost level, the spires are so named because of how they seem to rise up from the mountain beneath them and claw for the sky. On clear days, the crystalline deposits sparkle in each of the spires, reflecting the brilliant sunlight. Some legends say that the spires are actually a hand that is ready to catch Kahless should he fall from *Sto-Vo-Kor* back to the dominion of the living.

▲ **DIS lay'**

These "Caves of Promise," located deep beneath the mountain on which the monastery is built, are a complex network of tunnels carved by lava through the rock. According to *The Story of the Promise*, it's within these caves specifically that Kahless decreed he would one day be resurrected, a statement he apparently made after identifying Boreth as the planet of his return. In 2369, the monastery clerics who created the Kahless clone saw to it that his first appearance was here, in accordance with the legends, but they and many others still believe that the "true" first emperor will one day return. The largest cave, situated almost directly below the monastery itself, contains an ornamental fire pit that the clerics ensure burns continuously, as they believe it's by this light that Kahless will find his way from *Sto-Vo-Kor* back to the world of the living. Many of the clerics and other Klingons come here to meditate, perhaps hoping they will be the ones who will first behold Kahless's return.

SHOPPING AND ENTERTAINMENT

Aside from guided tours of the monastery and the surrounding grounds, the clerics don't spend a lot of time seeking ways to entertain tourists. The sole exception to this is a reading of *The Story of the Promise*, held each night at dusk in the monastery's main courtyard. As darkness encroaches, clerics take turns recounting by firelight the epic tale of how Kahless selected Boreth as the location of his inevitable return. Breaking with tradition and the formality that often surrounds readings of the *Story*, the performers here have adapted several passages to music and have even found ways to weave popular Klingon folk songs into the narrative, during which they invite the audience to sing along with the performers. At the conclusion of the recital, the performers make themselves available for questions regarding the *Story* and anything else visitors wish to ask about the monastery. Given their lives of isolation and solemn observance of protocol, the ministers and their staff seem to relish these opportunities to "come out of their shells" and interact with the audience. The nightly presentation usually makes for a pleasant way to round out a day's excursion before tourists return to their transport vessels.

▼ Sa' vIrurqu'law'

This general store began as a small medical clinic and pharmacy and has since grown to become the monastery's primary source for sundries and souvenirs. The actual clinic relocated to a larger chamber in the monastery decades ago, but many longtime residents still prefer to call the room by its original name, "the apothecary." Shoppers will find texts and other items pertaining to the monastery and its history, as well as different editions of *The Story of the Promise* and other historical and fictional tales featuring Kahless. It's also the only place where you'll find a selection of oven-baked *JInjoq* bread and freshly brewed *raktajino* coffee.

🍽 DINING

Aside from the dining facility on your chartered transport vessel, the only food options for travelers visiting Boreth are within the monastery itself. The clerics are known to hunt the indigenous wildlife for meat, in particular a large boar-like creature they have named the *nI' Ho'*, or simply, "long tooth." The meat from this beast is similar in flavor to saber bear or *targ*—especially when prepared by cooks as talented as those on staff here—and its long, sharp incisors are dense enough that the clerics and Jinvana groundskeepers are able to fashion them into serviceable bladed tools for maintaining the monastery grounds. Aside from the occasional *nI' Ho'* or other game hunt, the bulk of the meals here consist of fruits and vegetables grown on the monastery grounds. Some Klingon delicacies from Qo'noS are also imported weekly on a dedicated cargo vessel, but don't expect any of that fare if you opt to share a meal with the clerics. They like to save the limited portions of *gagh* and *pipius* claw for themselves.

TONG VEY

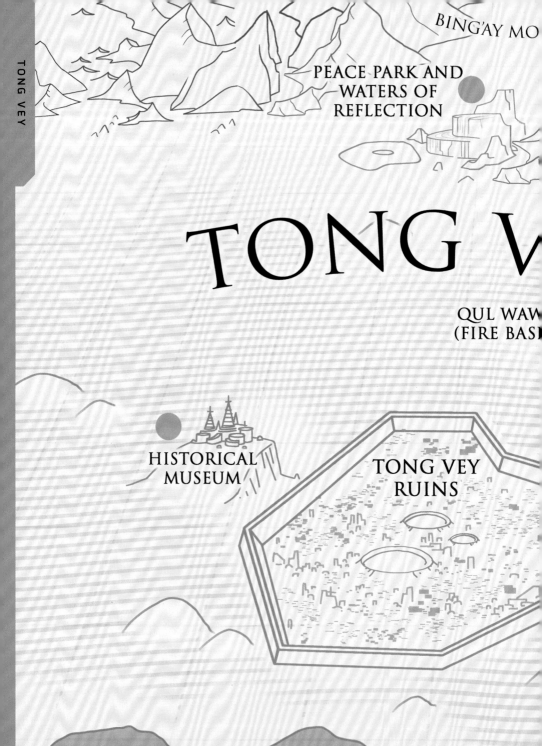

BING'AY MO

PEACE PARK AND
WATERS OF
REFLECTION

TONG V

QUL WAW
(FIRE BAS

HISTORICAL
MUSEUM

TONG VEY
RUINS

BIQ'A'BLNG OCEAN

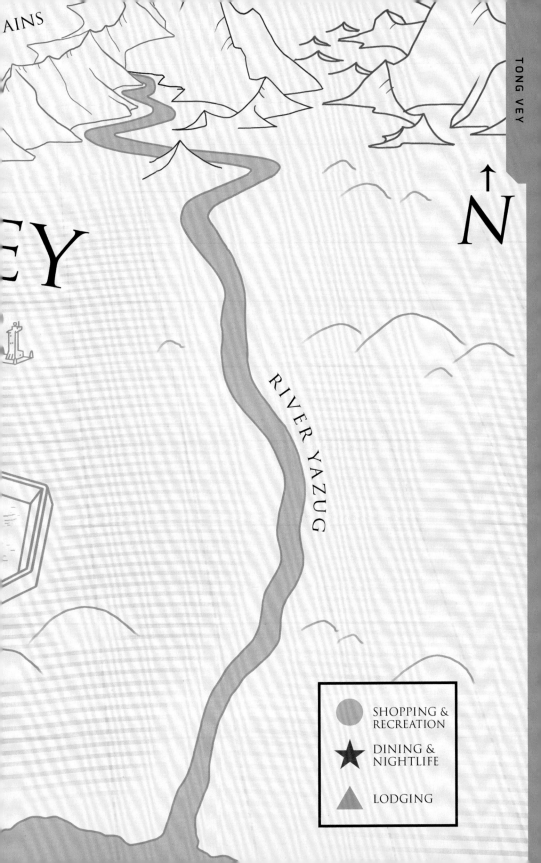

AINS

EY

N

RIVER YAZUG

SHOPPING & RECREATION

DINING & NIGHTLIFE

LODGING

POSSESSING A HISTORY THAT'S PERHAPS even more colorful than that of the First City, Tong Vey carries an unrivaled legacy of war and violence. Indeed, this ruined city was all but born from the fires of battle, and its death came in much the same fashion. Though once a hub of commerce and trade, it benefited from its favorable location on the continent's southern shores and proximity to the deepwater port that allowed access to and from the BIQ'a'blng Ocean. Later, as factions rose up to resist the efforts of the Empire to unite the Klingon people, Tong Vey became a sanctuary for these rebels.

After decades of resistance and numerous failed attempts to take the city, Tong Vey and its leader, the despot Kajahl, ultimately fell to the forces of Emperor Sompek, in the early years of his reign during the Second Dynasty. As punishment for generations of insolence and brazen attacks against the Empire, Sompek ordered every last person in the city put to death and the city itself reduced to rubble and ashes. To this day, it is unclear if the people of Tong Vey were united behind Kajahl against the Empire or if they were unwilling casualties of the dictator's unquenchable thirst for power.

Today, Tong Vey exists only as a vast landscape of crumbling ruins, along with a scattered collection of markers and small monuments, a museum, and the Dah poH (meaning "time of reckoning") battlefield, which has been designated a historical site. Scholars, historians, and curiosity seekers travel here to learn the full, stark truth of the city's history and the price it and its citizens paid for daring to stand against the Empire. Although destroying Tong Vey took a heavy toll on imperial forces, the message Sompek sent to other would-be rebels was unmistakable: Defy the Empire at your peril.

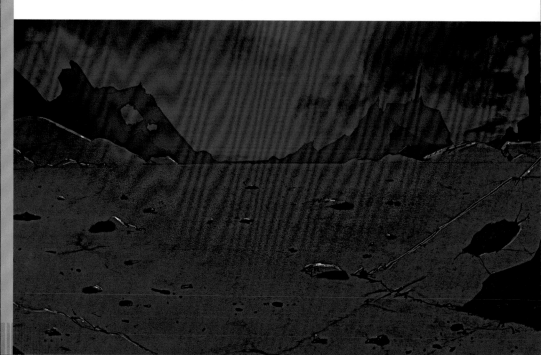

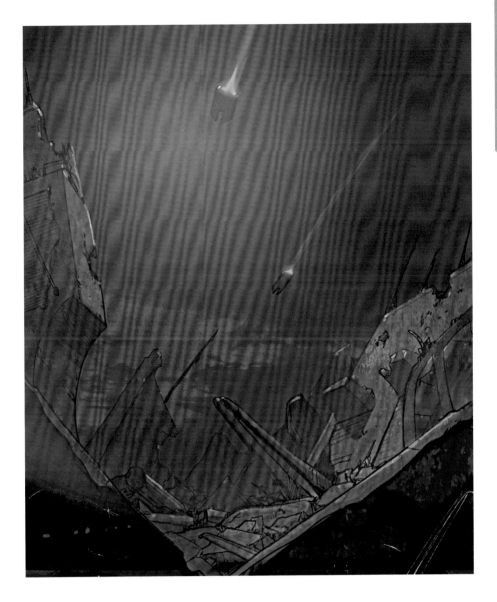

 GETTING AROUND

The city itself has been walled off to keep out the curious and prevent treasure hunters and looters from plundering the site. Security forces patrol the area in airborne skiffs. Visitors arrive via transport shuttles, which depart from most of the major cities on Qo'noS and come and go at sixty-minute intervals. Ground traffic in and around the historical areas is limited to pedestrian paths and mag-rail shuttles to and from the landing area as well as other outlying points of interest along the guided tour. The peace park and museum areas close at dusk, and the last transports depart thirty minutes after that.

WAR AND REGRETS

[First published in the 2268 Edition]
As I stand among what little remains of Tong Vey, I am reminded of its place as a dark chapter of history known to every Klingon warrior. I am referring not simply to the war itself, which was one of the bloodiest ground campaigns ever waged on the soil of Qo'noS, but also the events leading up to that final day of reckoning and the aftermath of the entire sordid affair. Generations of warrior candidates at the veS DuSaQ academy have studied and debated the battle, and the topic never fails to provoke passionate discussion, even when broached among elder soldiers such as myself. There are those who would prefer we not dwell on the past and instead focus our attention and energy on the future, but as anyone who has ever fought a war can tell you, it is of paramount importance to not just study and celebrate your victories, but also examine and learn from your failures so that you might apply harsh lessons to future engagements.

While the confrontation at Tong Vey was ultimately judged a success, it was still a loss—for Emperor Sompek, the Klingon people, and especially those who perished on the battlefield. However, Sompek could not permit such open insolence from Kajahl. I have heard it said, mostly in stories passed down between generations, that Sompek regretted the decree he made to annihilate the defeated city, and that he felt forced into his decision by a need to demonstrate to others that such willful disobedience and revolt could not be tolerated. Those same accounts say that the events of that day weighed upon Sompek for the remainder of his years.

There has not since been a campaign fought on Klingon soil as destructive as the Battle of Tong Vey, but the true cost of that conflict can only be appreciated by seeing it with your own eyes. Walking the Dah poH battlefield, which, even after all these generations, still bears the scars of prolonged fighting to which it bore witness, allows one to place the Empire's victory in its proper context. Though we triumphed, it is not a feat worthy of celebration. It was a battle that should never have been fought, provoked by a tyrant unworthy to be known as a Klingon, and ended by a warrior who would have preferred another path. We can only hope that future generations continue to heed the lessons of Tong Vey.

—General Korrd, Klingon Defense Force

SIGHTS AND ACTIVITIES

Given the city's status as a historical site, all activities here are aimed at educating visitors about the legacy of Tong Vey, including how it influenced future Klingon conflicts, both on Qo'noS and later as the Empire began its expansion to the stars. To that end, guided tours and marked paths allow visitors to reflect upon the costly battle waged here and the lives lost by those who paid the ultimate price for rebellion.

▼ Tong Vey Historical Museum

Despite his initial decrees that all evidence of the city or its inhabitants be forever expunged from Klingon history, Emperor Sompek was convinced by advisors not to allow the significance of this battle and its impact on the Empire to be forgotten, resulting in this single repository of artifacts, documents, and other items salvaged from the city's ruins. Thirteen exhibition galleries highlight the history of the city, beginning with its founding and early life as a trade hub, and continuing through its initial disputes with the First City and the Klingon High Council. The period in which Kajahl rises to rule the city and its neighboring regions is of course given significant space in the gallery, as are Emperor Sompek's decisions to attack, seize, and ultimately employ scorched-earth tactics against Tong Vey. The battle is well chronicled, with exhibits featuring numerous artifacts salvaged from the battlefield. A display of documents, maps, and other items seized from the leaders of Kajahl's armies paint a fascinating picture of the military tactics devised first to confront and later resist the Empire's attempts at expansion. A similar exhibit contrasts this campaign with the strategy employed by the forces of Sompek to bring this protracted conflict to its devastating end. Feel free to peruse the museum at your own pace, or opt for one of the guided tours.

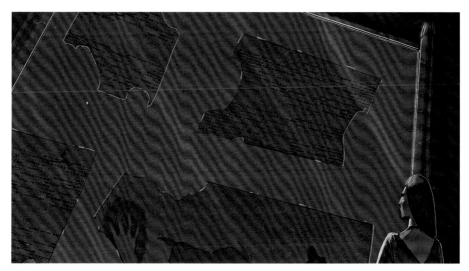

▼ Qul waw'

A "fire base," or early warning outpost, this was one of the few structures spared by Emperor Sompek following his order to have the entire city burned to the ground. According to accounts of the battle, this small encampment served as a forward operating post, used to direct fire for long-range artillery such as cannons and catapults against approaching enemy forces. Located approximately two kilometers north of the city ruins, the base quartered a medium-sized infantry division, which could be deployed as a rapid-response and blocking force in the event of invasion from the mountain passes to the north. Records from the Battle of Tong Vey show that the army directed by General Wri'suS and under Sompek's command made initial contact with Lord Kajahl's forces at the Qul waw' outpost. The dictator's forces were soon overrun as the incursion proceeded, and this loss set the tone for the rest of the campaign. Following the battle, Sompek decreed that this area, which marked the official start of the battle, be preserved. The outpost's stone walls remain relatively intact, along with portions of the interior living and working spaces. One area of the inner courtyard and adjoining buildings has been restored for display purposes, offering visitors insight into how life was lived at the outpost. Though you can walk to the site from the transport landing area, take one of the mag-rail shuttles so you'll have more time for sightseeing.

DID YOU KNOW?
THE BATTLE OF TONG VEY

Prior to the decisive conflict between the forces of Emperor Sompek and Kajahl, the renegade dictator had cemented his control over most of the continent's southern reaches under the counsel of seasoned warrior General Hjoh'pat. His realm included everything south of the BIng'av Mountains and north of the shores leading from the BIQ'a'blng Ocean. Those who disputed Kajahl's self-appointed role as absolute ruler of the region were dealt with quickly and harshly.

Kajahl might have been allowed to continue his reign for a time without fear of reprisal from the First City, but all of that changed when he began dispatching legions of Hjoh'pat's army into the northern reaches, beyond the mountains and toward the established trade routes between Quin'lat and the First City. With supply lines cut and Kajahl seizing goods and other valuables, a confrontation was inevitable. With Emperor Kaldon, the direct successor to Kahless, focused on securing territory and alliances in the northern regions, Kajahl's advances were left largely unchecked. It fell to Sompek, the third Klingon to assume the mantle of emperor, to deal with these increasingly audacious challenges to imperial authority. Indeed, Sompek was tested almost before he could sit on his throne, when forces loyal to Kajahl attempted to lay siege to the city of Quin'lat. Though that attack was repelled, Sompek knew that such outright impertinence could not go unanswered.

The new emperor dispatched ten thousand soldiers, commanded by veteran General Wri'suS, to seize Tong Vey once and for all. Though Hjoh'pat's forces attempted to counter the advance, even his superior numbers could not deal with the enveloping stratagem employed by Wri'suS and the launching of simultaneous assaults at multiple points along the city's perimeter. The smaller, more agile force—honed by Wri'suS through months of training and conditioning and using precepts handed down from the legendary military unit known as the Hand of Flame—was able to respond far more rapidly to the shifting situation and take advantage of the slower reaction time of Hjoh'pat's forces. Falling back after initial contact, and with enemy troops still reeling from the assault, the attacking forces would repeat the maneuver at new points of attack, further wearing already-strained defenders. By the end of the first day of fighting, imperial forces had broken through defensive fortifications on multiple fronts. Once inside the perimeter and able to move with speed behind Hjoh'pat's exhausted and demoralized troops, defeat came quickly to Tong Vey.

▼ Peace Park and Waters of Reflection

Situated in the foothills of the BIng'av Mountains to the north, the park affords visitors an unfettered view of the city remnants and the wall surrounding them. Though Emperor Sompek at first resisted the idea of any sort of commemoration of the battle or indeed any evidence that the city had even existed, he eventually relented to requests by scholars and citizens concerned that valuable lessons might be lost if Tong Vey and its story were allowed to fade from public memory. The peace park is a solemn place, offering silent tribute to those who died either during the battle or as a result of Sompek's merciless decree. Markers positioned around the grounds offer insight into the rule of Lord Kajahl and the events which precipitated Emperor Sompek's invasion. The gentle streams that run through the gardens here are conducive to meditation, flowing over rocks taken from the bed of the River Yazuq, which formed the city's eastern boundary and where many defeated Tong Vey soldiers were forcibly drowned in the aftermath of the battle. There are those who believe that the cascading waters in the park carry voices of the dead from the afterlife.

🛍 SHOPPING AND ENTERTAINMENT

Due to the somber nature of the site, there are no retail establishments beyond the small shop located inside the museum and the kiosks situated outside the peace park. The shop offers the usual assortment of books, recordings, and other materials, along with candles, which can be placed at designated markers within the peace park as part of an individual's meditation process.

Likewise, entertainment options are restricted to the museum's theater, which offers holorecordings of historical programs as well as fictionalized retellings of the battle. The recordings play on a rotating schedule, but visitors can also watch them individually at kiosks throughout the museum.

🍽 DINING AND NIGHTLIFE

Dining options around the historical site are limited to a pair of cafeterias on the museum's lower level. One of the facilities caters exclusively to Klingon warriors and other military personnel, while the other serves civilian Klingons as well as offworlders. Replicators are generally used for meal preparation, though a selection of handmade dishes from the cafeteria staff are always available. Note that, while bloodwine and other alcoholic beverages are available in the cafeteria serving the Klingon military visitors, such spirits are conspicuously absent from the other facility.

DID YOU KNOW?
THE HAND OF FLAME

Dismissed by many over the generations as being yet another exaggerated myth inspired by Kahless the Unforgettable, the elite fighting force known as the Hand of Flame has in recent years finally come to receive due respect and honor.

Led by three vaunted commanders, O'gat, Kollus, and To'Kar, the Hand of Flame began as a band of rebels opposed to the tyrant Molor's despotic regime during the time of Kahless. Each a master of a particular style of combat, this trio of veteran warriors combined their expertise and imparted it to their legions of soldiers, elevating the already formidable fighting skills of their troops to a whole new level. After teaching Kahless and his armies to defeat Molor, the Hand of Flame would go on to become one of the most celebrated fighting forces in the Empire's history, notching victories against the armies of rival factions who resisted attempts to unite the Klingon people.

Upon ascending to the throne, Emperor Sompek called upon the Hand to help him devise strategies for defeating Lord Kajahl. With the Hand's able assistance, Sompek and General Wri'suS were able to develop tactics that allowed their army to be more maneuverable and aggressive than Kajahl's forces, routing the defenders of Tong Vey within the first day of fighting.

The tactics of the Hand of Flame continue to be studied by academy students and seasoned warriors alike, and variations on their strategies have been employed by countless military commanders—with many of those battles ending in the same decisive manner as the Empire's victory at Tong Vey.

SEEK YOUR OWN *VENGEANCE!*

For the first time ever, you can be a part of the most exciting adventure in the Klingon Empire when you step into the world of *Battlecruiser Vengeance*! Only here, at this one-of-a-kind immersive attraction that employs state-of-the-art interactive holographic technology and a full cast of talented performers, can you lose yourself within the universe of the enduring and wildly popular entertainment series.

Step aboard the *Vengeance* as a member of its crew, answering the call to defend the Klingon Empire against all challengers and enemies. Interact with Captain Koth and his brave crew of warriors as the ship charges into battle, seeking honor and victory against the Empire's most renowned foes. Match wits with Captain James T. Kirk and the starship *Enterprise*. Triumph over Starfleet forces at the Battle of Donatu V, or the Romulan armada that attacked Narendra III. Forget the history texts: Ultimate Klingon victory is now in *your* hands!

Once you've defeated the Empire's enemies, relax with fellow Klingons and aliens from dozens of worlds at one of our premier taverns and restaurants, or purchase unique merchandise available nowhere else in the galaxy.

It's the ultimate *Battlecruiser Vengeance* experience, and you're right in the heart of it!

SEEK YOUR OWN
VENGEANCE!

Coming Summer 2388
Po'liDa District, Quin'lat

INSIGHT EDITIONS

PO Box 3088
San Rafael, CA 94912
www.insighteditions.com

 Find us on Facebook: www.facebook.com/InsightEditions

Follow us on Twitter: @insighteditions

Library of Congress Cataloging-in-Publication Data available.

ISBN: 978-1-60887-519-1

Publisher: Raoul Goff
Acquisitions Manager: Robbie Schmidt
Art Director: Chrissy Kwasnik
Designer: Ashley Quackenbush
Executive Editor: Vanessa Lopez
Senior Editor: Chris Prince
Managing Editor: Alan Kaplan
Production Editor: Elaine Ou
Production Manager: Alix Nicholaeff

 REPLANTED PAPER

ACKNOWLEDGMENTS

Thanks once again to John Van Citters at CBS Consumer Products and Chris Prince at Insight Editions for inviting me back to write this second *Hidden Universe: Star Trek* travel guide. As with the Vulcan edition, working on this was another opportunity to further my experience and appreciation for how these "art heavy" books come together. Yes, it was a lot of work, but it was also a lot of fun, and therefore the work was worth it.

Many, many thanks to art director Chrissy Kwasnik, designer Ashley Quackenbush, and artists Livio Ramondelli and Peter Markowski. The artwork you'll find among these pages does a magnificent job of propping up my pithy text, making this an eye-catching tome for hardcore fans and casual readers alike. This book is all the better for their creations and exceptional efforts, and they have my undying gratitude.

As with the Vulcan travel guide, I consulted a number of sources while pulling this book together, including several novels and other *Star Trek* "reference works" published over the years. Even if I only made brief mention of some factoid or interesting tidbit I discovered within one of these books, websites, or other sources, I raise my glass in appreciation of the authors and other dedicated people involved in their publication.

Finally, and as always, the last bit of thanks is for my wife and daughters, who continue to support my writerly shenanigans while making sure I'm fed and loved while working on projects like this, and then letting me sleep in once I've hit the deadline and the coma takes hold.

SOURCES

Carter, Carmen. *Star Trek: The Next Generation: The Devil's Heart*. New York: Pocket Books, 1993.
DeCandido, Keith R. A. *Star Trek: I.K.S. Gorkon: A Good Day to Die*. New York: Pocket Books, 2003.
———. *Star Trek: I.K.S. Gorkon: Honor Blade*. New York: Pocket Books, 2003.
———. *Star Trek: The Klingon Art of War*. New York: Gallery Books, 2014.
Ford, John M. *Star Trek: The Final Reflection*. New York: Pocket Books, 1984.
Ford, John M., Guy W. McLimore Jr., Greg K. Poehlein, David F. Tepool. *The Klingons*. FASA Corporation, 1983.
Friedman, Michael Jan. *Star Trek: The Next Generation: Kahless*. New York: PocketBooks, 1997.
———. *Star Trek: New Worlds, New Civilizations*. New York: Pocket Books, 1999.
Okrand, Marc. *Star Trek: The Klingon Way*. New York: Pocket Books, 1996.
———. *Star Trek: Klingon for the Galactic Traveler*. New York: Pocket Books, 1997.
Ward, Dayton. *Star Trek: In the Name of Honor*. New York: Pocket Books, 2002.

Memory Alpha wiki. http://memory-alpha.org

Memory Beta wiki. http://memory-beta.wikia.com